Henry W Rugg

The Presidents of the United States

Sketches

Henry W Rugg

The Presidents of the United States
Sketches

ISBN/EAN: 9783337404109

Printed in Europe, USA, Canada, Australia, Japan

Cover: Foto ©Andreas Hilbeck / pixelio.de

More available books at **www.hansebooks.com**

THE PRESIDENTS OF THE UNITED STATES ❖❖ SKETCHES BY HENRY W. RUGG, D. D.

Illustrated

BY TWENTY-TWO PORTRAITS.

PREFACE.

My purpose has been, in preparing these sketches, to tell the story of each President's life, directing attention to the distinguishing features of his character and the more important events of his career. It will be understood that this work can only present a summary of these movements and incidents, for the full narration of which many volumes would be required. My endeavor has been to be accurate in the record given, at the same time striving to make the biographies as readable, symmetrical and well balanced as their condensed form would allow. In conformity with this thought, care has been taken that all data of historical statements should be reliable; that the individuality of each biographical subject should be made conspicuous; that a proper emphasis should be placed upon the lessons naturally associated with the records of patriotic endeavor and wise statesmanship.

In studying the lives of the Presidents, there is made apparent not only the greatness of these honored men, but the fact of the Nation's progress as it has gathered to itself more and more the conditions and elements of an enduring strength.

H. W. RUGG.

List of Illustrations.

—

CONTENTS.

6 CONTENTS.

ANDREW JACKSON.

MARTIN VAN BUREN.

WILLIAM HENRY HARRISON.

JOHN TYLER.

JAMES KNOX POLK.

ZACHARY TAYLOR.

MILLARD FILLMORE.

FRANKLIN PIERCE.

CONTENTS.

GEORGE WASHINGTON.

FIRST PRESIDENT OF THE UNITED STATES.

GEORGE WASHINGTON.

BOYHOOD LIFE AND SURROUNDINGS — RESPONSIBILITIES EARLY ASSUMED — THE
YOUNG COMMANDER — MILITARY SERVICES DURING THE FRENCH WAR —
DOMESTIC LIFE — AMERICAN REVOLUTION — COMMANDER-IN-CHIEF OF COLO-
NIAL ARMY — WASHINGTON AS GENERAL — CLOSE OF THE WAR — PRESIDENT
OF THE FEDERAL CONVENTION — PRESIDENT OF THE UNITED STATES —
CLOSING SCENES AT MOUNT VERNON — SUMMARY OF CHARACTER.

THE hero, like his humbler brother, cannot choose his
birthplace. The great man, however, may make the
place of his birth what he will by virtue of its association with his genius and fame, for the most unattractive spot
on earth may thus arouse a human interest more wide-spread
and abiding than any sentiment inspired by mere beauty of
situation or surroundings. So it is that the tract of land on
Bridge's Creek, in old Virginia, has a charm for the American, and many another, because here, in the one-story farm-
house overlooking the Potomac, was born, February 22, 1732,
George Washington, the first President of our United States.
The homestead has disappeared, but the place in Westmoreland County where the famous general was a "baby new to
earth and sky" is still pointed out to the inquiring traveler.
The family removed from this farm-house soon after the new
life had been added to the circle, to another farm near Fredericksburg, and on high ground overlooking the waters of the

Rappahannock River.   Here and at Mount Vernon, then owned by his half brother, Lawrence Washington, and at Belvoir, the home of William Fairfax, all situated comparatively near together and close to Fredericksburg, the lad spent his boyhood days.   The youth, George Washington, was very much as other boys are, if a pure-minded, healthy, intelligent lad be a type.   He lived an out-door life, had a perfect physical being, a manly frame and bearing, and added to this was a training of books and the influence of a refined home, so that the boy, while lacking some of the advantages offered the youth of to-day, had much to help him in his preparation for the future, whatever that might bring.   Doubtless his admiration for William Fairfax, and the frequency with which he visited that cultured home, instilled into his heart a love for books and study, and a desire to form a literary style as correct and polished as that of his friend, who had been a comrade of Addison and a contributor to the columns of the *Spectator*. Washington could never have been the great man he was, had not this foundation been laid; and his country and the world owe a debt of gratitude to his family and friends who trained the boyish frame and the boyish mind to meet the trials and the emergencies which great leaders are called to endure.

Washington was not long allowed to remain a boy; he took upon himself responsibilities at an early age.   Lord Fairfax, owning vast lands, unexplored, in the region around the Blue Ridge Mountains, suggested that young Washington should make a survey of the district and report its condition.   This was done, and he gained much knowledge concerning the country, Indian life, and many other things useful in the warfare and campaigns which followed.   Then came the time when a person was chosen to be sent on a mission to the French outposts and among the Indians on the frontier, and Governor Dinwiddie selected George Washington, though he had but recently attained his majority. The mission required discretion, courage, and skill on the part of its leader, and the demand was met. The young man showed tact and wisdom, and the expedition, perilous to the extreme, was successful, besides revealing the capabilities and powers of the man, and preparing him by another step for his life-work.

The French aggressions continued throughout the year 1754, and Colonel Washington, in command of Virginia troops, rendered excellent service, displaying military genius and the essential qualities of successful leadership, remarkable in a young man but twenty-two years of age. Declining the chief command, Washington volunteered as aide, and accompanied General Braddock on his expeditions. This English officer, a man of some renown, and possessed of much technical military knowledge, was utterly unskilled in the methods of Indian warfare, and being somewhat opinionated, listened to no advice, and pursued his own plans, so unsuitable to the country and the foes to be encountered. Washington warned Braddock against the dangers of Indian ambuscades, but the warning of the colonial colonel was unheeded, and when the English army was near Fort Duquesne, on the shore of the Monongahela River, July 9, 1755, Braddock's command was surprised by the French and Indians, and suffered a terrible and humiliating defeat, Braddock himself being killed and the greater part of his officers killed or wounded. Washington showed great courage and skill, seeming to bear a charmed life, for bullets passed through his garments and two horses were shot under him, leaving him unhurt. By his coolness after the catastrophe, he saved the forces from absolute ruin, and practically assumed command of the disorganized remnant of the troops. Soon after, Governor Dinwiddie, never very friendly to Washington, appointed him commander of the Virginia forces, and he remained in command until the close of the

French and Indian War. During this part of his military career he met with many troubles, could not carry out his desired plans, suffered in bodily health, endured hardships and fatigue, was misunderstood and at variance with Governor Dinwiddie and others. He yet proved himself a distinguished military leader, and was the most popular officer in Virginia. The victory of Wolfe at Quebec, September 13, 1759, practically closed the French war, and ended for a time Washington's military career.

In the midst of this busy existence Washington found time to woo and win a wife, the beautiful Mrs. Custis, of Virginia. They were married January 6, 1759, and soon after took possession of Mount Vernon, where they resided for nearly sixteen years, probably the happiest period of Washington's life. Although fond of out-door living and agricultural pursuits, it must not be inferred that Washington withdrew himself from all public affairs and patriotic interests. During all the time of his so-called retirement from political life, he was a member of the House of Burgesses and associated with Patrick Henry and other foremost patriots in resisting the claims of Great Britain. England, however, paid no attention to these warnings, and soon the situation became serious, and armed resistance was necessary. In 1774, the first Continental Congress was convened at Philadelphia, and the year following George Washington, representing Virginia, was unanimously elected commander-in-chief of the American Army, forces having already been gathered and blood already shed in the cause of American Independence.

Washington accepted the responsible position to which he was called, and proceeded as expeditiously as possible to Cambridge, Massachusetts, where, under the shadow of the great elm, now standing, he read his commission and assumed command of the American forces. It is difficult to sum up in a few words his conduct and generalship during the war, which lasted between eight and nine years. No meteor flashes of military glory make Washington's name famous. His was the steady courage, the facing of all obstacles, the unassuming yet determined action, the just dealings, which made the true man and the true soldier, the successful general and the Nation's hero. He was criticised, as all reformers and leaders must be; he had no wealthy government, and but few supplies of war to aid in his movements; he had to contend with ignorance and incapacity on every side, with jealousies of his associates and the interference of Congress. It was the thousand small victories instead of the one grand triumph, the unwavering patriotism and forgetfulness of self, that made George Washington the hero and the leader, whose name the American people reverence, and all other nations respect.

The war of the Revolution virtually came to an end with the surrender of Cornwallis at Yorktown, October 19, 1783. The closing scene of the war was the withdrawal of the British troops from New York, November 25, 1783. A few days later Washington took farewell of his troops, and in the course of a fortnight formally surrendered his commission as general to the Congress then sitting at Annapolis, Maryland. In accepting the resignation, the president of the Congress, in his address to Washington, closed with these prophetic words: "The glory of your virtues will descend to remotest generations."

At the close of the war Washington retired to Mount Vernon, and lived there a quiet, peaceful life for nearly three years, all the time keeping up his interest in American politics and watching the struggles of the young nation to establish a form of government. At last affairs were in such a condition, that a convention composed of delegates from the states was held at Philadelphia, and Washington represented Virginia, as a matter of course. He was made president of this convention, which framed the Constitution of the United States. The year following he was elected President of the Nation, and was inaugurated in New York, April 30, 1789. He was re-elected in 1792, and served eight years as President, refusing re-election for the third term, as he felt unable to bear longer the trials and duties of a public life. His administration showed a wise statesmanship at a time when the Nation was testing a new form of government, and there were many difficulties in the way. The Pennsylvania riots, the Indian troubles along the frontier, the influence of the French Revolution, the criticism and distrust, oftentimes, with which he was regarded by his countrymen, these, and many other troubles came upon Washington, and with all his courage and steadfastness, it is reported that he once said in desperation: "I would rather be in my grave than be President of the United States." At the close of his administration affairs were comparatively smooth in the land, but it has remained for later years to testify of the wise judgment and the firm hand which guided and ruled our Nation in its infancy, and placed it upon such a foundation of permanence and strength.

In the year 1797, on the 3d of March, Washington gave a farewell dinner to his friends, and among the distinguished guests were the newly-elected President, John Adams, and his wife. Washington at once went to his home at Mount Vernon, and for a brief time enjoyed the tranquil pleasures of a country life in the place he loved so well. His domestic life was singularly happy, and was a soothing balm for the many trials endured in his public career. Death came to him quickly, as he would have chosen, for, with a brief illness of only forty-eight hours, the glorious spirit sought its new and better home, after having "fought a good fight" here on earth and being entitled to the rest and glories of the immortal state. Washington died at Mount Vernon, December 14, 1799.

A thoughtful and just estimate of the character of George Washington reveals a man having the right balance of mind, more valuable as an attribute of successful leadership than brilliant traits of one kind offsetting defects and lack of character in one form or another. Washington's faculties and attributes were evenly developed, and his greatness did not lie in any one form of achievement. He had a noble purpose, a confidence in his own judgment, and while he listened to advice from others, and consulted the accumulated wisdom of the world, he carried out his own plans in the face of all opposition, if they seemed to him best for the prosperity of his beloved nation. Washington had many traits of character which endeared him to those around him, and make his memory precious to the American people. He was manly, and not effeminate; he was true and straight-forward, knowing no deceit and capable of no subterfuges; he was an angler and a hunter, a polished writer and a statesman, a genial host, an agreeable companion, and an affectionate husband and father. When history writes and shall write her praise of George Washington, as President and General, she need not shun the open page that tells of his home life, nor cover it with charity; but she may picture the rounded, symmetrical man, the well-balanced mind, and the life, crowded with duties, yet showing no neglected talents.

JOHN ADAMS.

SECOND PRESIDENT OF THE UNITED STATES.

JOHN ADAMS.

PRESIDENT, MARCH 4, 1797 — MARCH 4, 1801.

BIRTHPLACE AND ANCESTRY — HIS COURSE AS A STUDENT — TEACHES SCHOOL IN
WORCESTER, MASSACHUSETTS — PRACTICES LAW IN BOSTON — CHAMPIONS THE
CAUSE OF LIBERTY — MARRIAGE AND DOMESTIC LIFE — CONNECTION WITH
INDEPENDENCE — COMMISSIONER TO FRANCE — VICE-PRESIDENT UNDER WASH-
INGTON — ELECTED PRESIDENT — HIS ADMINISTRATION — RETURN TO QUINCY
— PERSONAL WORTH AND CHARACTER.

MASSACHUSETTS has furnished two Presidents of the
United States, John Adams and John Quincy Adams,
father and son. The old town of Quincy was the birthplace of both, although when the elder Adams was born, October 30, 1735, the settlement formed a part of Braintree, and so
remained till incorporated under the name of Quincy, in 1792.
John Adams, the second President of this Republic, inherited
something of firmness and strength of character from his father,
a hard-working, God-fearing man, and from his earlier ancestors, Henry Adams and John Alden, both prominent among the
Pilgrim founders of New England. Brought up with farmers,
and living an out-door life, the boy became impressed with the
idea that he would follow agricultural pursuits, and would not
spend his life among books and in the seclusion of a library.
A few days of hard work on the farm, even in the midst of the
natural beauties which had so attracted him in his hours of idleness, satisfied the lad, and he was quite willing to go to school,

where he applied himself diligently to his studies, so that he
entered Harvard College when sixteen years old, graduating
four years later with a record for ability as a student and for
straightforward and manly characteristics. Having received a
good education, all that the father was able to give the young
man, he must now support himself and lean upon his own
resources.   He studied law in Worcester, Massachusetts, and
paid his expenses by teaching school.   He was admitted to the
bar of Suffolk County in 1758, and began the practice of law in
his native town soon after, showing early in his career ability in
his profession, and acquiring a reputation for his talents as a clear
thinker and able counsel.   Devoted to his profession, young
Adams spent some of rare leisure in wooing Miss Abigail
Smith, of Weymouth, whom he married in October, 1764.
This clergyman's daughter possessed the qualities of a noble
womanhood, and was a helpmeet to her husband in every
sense of the word.   The name of Abigail Adams is honored
and respected, not only because she was the wife of the illustrious President, but by reason of her womanly graces, her
rare force of character, and her intellectual and moral endow-
ments.

Shortly after his marriage he removed to Boston, where
wider fields were opened to him for the exercise of his abilities
as lawyer and citizen.   At this period the exactions of England
upon the American colonies became intolerable, and Adams,
who had always maintained his interest in public affairs, came
to the front as a patriot, and, in company with James Otis and
other distinguished men, held councils as to what course their
country should pursue in resisting the arbitrary encroachments
of Great Britain.   His first prominent connection with a movement to resist England's hard rule was at a public meeting
held in Braintree to oppose the Stamp Act.   Adams, whose
writings had already excited favorable comment for their liter-

ary style and clear presentation of subjects discussed, prepared and offered resolutions condemning the act. These resolutions were unanimously adopted, and were so timely and forcible, and so well expressed the popular feeling, that forty other towns in Massachusetts adopted them without a single change.

Although Adams was an ardent patriot, he was large-minded and tolerant; several of his acts at this period show both his natural force of character and that he did not blindly follow the popular will. After the Boston Massacre, in 1770, he acted as one of the counsel to defend Captain Preston, who ordered the soldiers to fire upon the citizens of Boston, and Mr. Adams was of course censured by the populace. Although criticised by many, he was generally popular, as before, and was sent as representative from the town of Boston to the Massachusetts Legislature. He held to his bold convictions and antagonized many of the measures of the Provincial governor, Hutchinson, while serving in the legislature, and continued to write able articles for the press, condemning the course pursued by the British Government. In 1774 he was appointed to represent Massachusetts in the Continental Congress at Philadelphia, where he took foremost rank as an able advocate of liberty, a leader well equipped for his position. His mind had grasped already the idea of independence, but the people were not ready for it, and popular feeling was against those, Adams among the number, supposed to be in sympathy with the thought. England showed no disposition to relent; Boston Harbor was filled with armed ships, and the port was closed; and Adams and a few others felt that no longer was it a question of redress of grievances: it was time for independence. In 1775 Mr. Adams successfully used his influence in Congress to procure the appointment of Washington as commander-in-chief, and the next year he was called to aid in the framing of the Declaration of Independence. Although Jefferson drafted the important document, it was John Adams who supported it in Congress with so much of eloquence and power. Jefferson wrote of his friend and colleague: "The great pillar of support to the Declaration of Independence, and its ablest advocate and champion in Congress was John Adams." How Adams himself regarded the Declaration and the results sure to follow, is shown by a letter which he wrote to his wife on the day following its adoption: "Yesterday, the greatest question was decided that was ever debated in America; a greater, perhaps, never was or will be decided among men. A resolution was passed that these United States are, and ought to be, free and independent states. The 4th of July, 1776, will be a memorable epoch in the history of America. I am well aware of the toil and blood and treasure that it will cost to maintain this Declaration, and support and defend these states; yet through all the gloom I can see that the end is worth more than all the means, and that posterity will triumph, though you and I may rue, which I hope we shall not."

In December of 1777, Mr. Adams was appointed commissioner to the court of France in place of Silas Deane, recalled. In February of '78 he embarked on the frigate *Boston*, to undertake as soon as possible the duties imposed. The voyage was made in rough and stormy weather, and was an eventful and perilous trip. Several British ships were sighted, and the *Boston* gave chase to and captured one, which proved to be a privateer, the *Martha*, carrying fourteen guns. It is said that Mr. Adams took part in this engagement, carrying a musket, and doing excellent service, till he was forcibly removed from danger by his friends. Although Mr. Adams was respected in France, he showed little talent for diplomacy, and his dignity, his stiff manners, and unflinching honesty were not offset by the tact of a skillful embassador. Franklin had already concluded a treaty of alliance with France, and by his gracious bearing had made himself popular in the country where so much attention was paid to the politeness and the minor courtesies of social life. In 1779 Adams returned to his native land, and found congenial occupation in helping frame the new state constitution of Massachusetts. While he was engaged in this work he was appointed minister to Great Britain for the purpose of negotiating a treaty of peace and commerce. He reached Paris in 1780, and finding much to annoy him in the motives which caused France to enter into the American alliance, and, feeling himself alienated from the views held by Franklin, Adams decided to go to Holland, where he worked successfully to establish an alliance of amity and commerce. Holland recognized the United States as a free and independent nation, and Adams, as its acknowledged minister, was welcomed in the diplomatic bodies of The Hague. He also succeeded in obtaining large sums of money as loans for his country from the bankers of Amsterdam. Returning to Paris, he was associated with Franklin, Jay, and Laurens in a commission to conclude treaties with the several countries of Europe ; and under their direction, Adams rendering important aid, the treaty of peace with Great Britain was signed September 3, 1783, the provisional treaty having been agreed to November 30, 1782. The services which Adams rendered for his country during the war of the Revolution were no less important in the light of history than those of Washington, though they were of a different character. Of this "Washington of negotiation," one of his biographers says: "As we ascend the mount of history, and rise above the vapors of party prejudice, we shall all acknowledge that we owe our independence more to John Adams than to any other created being, and that he was the great leader of the American Revolution."

Peace having been proclaimed, Mr. Adams was appointed minister to Great Britain to represent the Republic of the United States, an office justly held to demand the utmost ability and discretion. At that time, 1785, he was living in Paris, but at once crossed the channel to assume the arduous and delicate responsibilities imposed. He met with a courteous reception from the king, but felt himself hampered in thought and action, and soon asked leave to return to his own country, coming back in 1788, and receiving from Congress recognition and thanks for his services. He then repaired to his home, applying himself to professional and literary pursuits, and sought to encourage art, science, and letters. In that same year he was given honorable preferment by being chosen Vice-President, and in that office he was closely associated with Washington during the eight years of his administration. At its close, after a hotly-contested election, Adams was chosen President, and inaugurated at Philadelphia, March 4, 1797.

The administration of John Adams is more justly estimated in the light of history with the progress of years, and a proper value is placed upon the man, his strict integrity of purpose and life. He was never very popular among his contemporaries, though many of them realized his worth and patriotism. He did not know how to conciliate his party or personal opponents, and the four years of his administration were years of struggle and trial. The French Revolution caused strife among the American patriots, and they became alienated from each other because of their intense partisanship with either France or England. Some of Mr. Adams' measures were successful, however, and he maintained the dignity of his country among the foreign powers. He served only four years, being defeated at the election in 1801, when Jefferson was chosen President, being more popular than Adams on account of his more tolerant and sympathetic views. Mr. Adams retired to his home in Quincy, and lived there till the time of his death. He maintained, throughout his long life, the full possession of his mental faculties, and enjoyed reviewing his triumphs and living them over again in the successes of his son, John Quincy Adams. In 1818 the noble wife who had shared the sorrows and joys of her husband for over half a century passed away, and the eight years longer which Mr. Adams spent on the earth were tinged with a sadness never quite overcome. On the 4th of July, 1826, his mortal career was ended, and that same day is made memorable by the death of Thomas Jefferson, his friend and fellow-worker for the principles of independence.

The outward attractions of gracious manners and magnetic personality, John Adams never possessed. The sterling qualities of his inner self rang true in every instance, however, and the "Duke of Braintree," as he was frequently termed, was a man to rule, and, by force of his powerful intellect and his judicial mind, to sway the destinies of a nation. He was something of a scholar, and a writer of considerable skill and elegance of expression. His family were very dear to his heart, and his friends, once gained, enjoyed his confidence and esteem ever after. Many there are who can be courteous and genial; few who can possess the enduring virtues which made John Adams capable of doing so much for his country, and his own deeply-imbued principles of right and justice. History dismisses with a single word, and oblivion hides the man whose claim for attention is a gracious manner, while true merit is always acknowledged, if but slowly, and wins an ever-deepening regard from a world that, in spite of all its follies and errors, respects virtue and truth wherever found. So the generations of the American people reverence the name of John Adams, an honest gentleman, and a clear thinker; an able writer, and a conscientious President of the United States.

THOMAS JEFFERSON.

THIRD PRESIDENT OF THE UNITED STATES.

THOMAS JEFFERSON.

PRESIDENT, MARCH 4, 1801 — MARCH 4, 1809.

BOYHOOD — A CULTURED HOME — HELPFUL INFLUENCES AND SURROUNDINGS — AN
ARDENT STUDENT — A SUCCESSFUL ADVOCATE — RESIDENCE AT MONTI-
CELLO — MARRIAGE — MEMBER OF THE GENERAL CONGRESS — AUTHOR
OF DECLARATION OF INDEPENDENCE — GOVERNOR OF VIRGINIA — SECRE-
TARY OF STATE — VICE-PRESIDENT — PRESIDENT FOR EIGHT YEARS —
CLOSING SCENES — RECORD FOR ABILITY AND SERVICE.

THE thoughts of manhood always return in fond remembrance to childhood's home and surroundings, and it is
a cause for congratulation when such memories bring to
mind the outward beauties of natural scenery and the tender
recollections of a happy family gathered under the sheltering
roof-tree. So the lad, Thomas Jefferson, born April 2, 1743,
in Shadwell, Albemarle County, Virginia, must have been
influenced by the attractive scenes which met his view, the far-
reaching undulations of the Blue Ridge Mountains, the encir-
cling forests and the peaceful valleys and slopes of a well-
cared-for and prosperous farming district. The home was a
cultured one for those times, the husband and father, Peter
Jefferson, possessing some wealth and considerable education;
quite a prominent man in the hamlet where he lived, and believing in the helps of acquired knowledge for his children.
Thus the boy Thomas Jefferson was encouraged in his studious tendencies, had a private tutor for Greek and Latin,
and was well-prepared to enter an advanced class in William
and Mary College in 1760, graduating from that institution in

3

1762, when but nineteen years of age. The quiet youth pursued his studies in an earnest love for the acquirement of knowledge, and had a rare faculty for the languages, an almost equal ability for science and mathematics, so that his mind was well-balanced and equipped for mature efforts. Having many advantages of position, and the wealth to make his college life a gay one, Jefferson was a student from the love of learning, and his simple, regular habits, his upright principles, his courteous manners, early developed, characterized him throughout his entire life.

When Jefferson decided to enter the legal profession he began the study of law with Mr. George Wythe, then holding foremost rank among the lawyers of Virginia. Jefferson was admitted to practice in 1767, and won immediate success at the bar. Although possessing a weak voice and an unimpressive manner, which kept him from being an effective and eloquent speaker, he had the quick perceptions, the power of application, the learning, which made him a skillful and successful advocate, as he soon came to be regarded among the profession and elsewhere. He acquired some means in the practice of law, thus adding to the considerable property which had been left him by his father, who died in 1757. Thus he prospered, until the plantation of 1,900 acres, which came to him by inheritance, was increased in 1774 to 5,000 acres, owned without incumbrance.

Jefferson's public life may be said to have begun with his election to the House of Burgesses in 1768, an office which he continued to fill by repeated elections until the Provincial Legislature was closed by the Revolution. Before his election to the House of Burgesses, he had been aroused by the oppressions of the British government in dealing with the American colonies, and was ready to aid in a resistance of the mother country to the utmost of his ability. When a law student, in 1765, he had listened to Patrick Henry's celebrated speech against the Stamp Act, in the Virginia House of Delegates, and from that time he was committed heart and soul to the cause of American independence and linked to the band of patriots in Virginia and Massachusetts, working so enthusiastically for their country's rights. His first decisive action of a public nature was taken in 1769, when the governor dissolved the Virginia Legislature five days after its organization, and the members, Jefferson among them, meeting in a hall, signed their names to a document, agreeing to stand together and co-operate with Massachusetts in her resistance of the Stamp Act.

During the next two or three years Jefferson was busily occupied in preparing a residence at Monticello, a beautifully situated home, afterwards a historic place, whose walls ever held a reputation for the graceful and abundant hospitalities of its owner. On the first day of the year, 1772, Mr. Jefferson married Mrs. Martha Skelton, a beautiful, highly-accomplished, and wealthy widow of Williamsburg, Virginia.

The events that gave rise to the American Revolution followed each other in quick succession. Great Britain continued her harsh measures in dealing with the colonies, and so encouraged the growing feeling of resistance in the hearts of the people. The patriotic leaders in the new world, Jefferson among the number, at first thought to avoid an actual conflict of arms with England, but when it was seen that war was inevitable, these men were soon convinced that the colonies must make a bold push for freedom. As early as 1774 Jefferson was in correspondence with able patriots, advocating the making of a common cause by the colonies in vigorously resisting the pretensions of the British Crown. At this time and shortly after, when the crisis was still impending, he wrote and published several notable articles bearing upon the condition of affairs in his country.

Under the intensified feeling aroused by the passage of the Boston Port Bill and the harsh enforcement of its provisions, a convention was called in Virginia to consider and act upon the alarming situation. Jefferson, who was a member of this body, gave intelligent advice which was regarded in almost every action that was taken. He was soon after elected to the General Congress then sitting at Philadelphia, taking his seat in June, 1775, eight days after Colonel George Washington had been chosen Commander-in-Chief of the American armies.

Jefferson soon identified himself with the measures and movements in that Congress, which culminated in the Declaration of Independence. As the coercive action of England increased, the delegates in Congress, together with their constituents generally, felt more in favor of independence. After the battle of Lexington, April 19, 1775, the common feeling became manifest that there was only one course to pursue — the Colonies must strike for complete freedom and seek to establish a nation. Congress had already passed a resolution declaring "that these United Colonies are, and of right ought to be, free and independent States," and soon a committee was appointed to draft a resolution in accordance therewith. This committee was composed of Thomas Jefferson, John Adams, Benjamin Franklin, Roger Sherman, and Robert R. Livingston. Jefferson wrote the declaration, though a few of its sentences were suggested by other members of the committee. It was adopted July 4, 1776, and received throughout the country with great rejoicing.

Jefferson participated in efforts to reorganize the Government of the Confederation, and prosecute the war of independence to a successful issue. He was an important factor on the American side in the long, hard contest. At the darkest period he was elected governor of Virginia, succeeding Patrick Henry. Soon after Virginia suffered greatly from the English troops that, with General Tarleton in command, were seeking to capture Governor Jefferson, at Monticello. He escaped, but his estates at Elk Hill were seized by the enemy and left a waste. The conduct of Jefferson, as governor, was criticised in many respects, but it has been shown that he tried to act in harmony with Washington's policy ; and on his retirement, the thanks of the Assembly were voted him in acknowledgment of his services while holding the gubernatorial office.

In 1782, he was appointed member of a commission to negotiate a treaty with Great Britain, but the negotiations advanced so rapidly that he was not called to go abroad; he reported in Congress the next year the treaty, which was shortly afterwards ratified. During the year 1784 he visited several of the capitals of Europe, and was associated with Adams and Franklin in attempting negotiations, efforts which were not at the time completely successful. In March, 1785, he succeeded Dr. Franklin at the Court of France, retaining the position till 1789, when he returned to the United States, entering, the year following, upon the duties of Secretary of State in Washington's Cabinet, a position which he held till December 31, 1793. At that time he resigned the office and retired to private life at Monticello. While Secretary he antagonized many of the measures approved by the President, especially those originated by Mr. Hamilton, Secretary of the Treasury, between whom and himself there were great differences of opinion on political matters. Mr. Jefferson led the opposition to the Federal Administration, and helped form the party called Republican by its friends, and Democratic by its enemies. In 1796, he was candidate for the presidency against John Adams; the latter was elected, and Jefferson was inaugurated as Vice-President, March 4, 1797. In 1800, Jefferson was again nominated for the presidency and, after a hotly-contested campaign, was successful; he was inaugurated at Washington as third President of the United States, March 4, 1801. He was re-elected to a second term, serving eight years in all, and conducting an administration marked by signal events, and by increasing prosperity and progress throughout the country.

Among the important events which illumine the administration of Jefferson are the closing of the African slave-trade, the extermination of the Algerine pirates, the exploration and development of the Western territories, and especially the purchase of Louisiana. President Jefferson was greatly criticised by his contemporaries for his course in buying this vast tract of land, including a region of nearly nine hundred thousand square miles, extending westward from the Mississippi to the Rocky Mountains and northward from Mexico to British America. The President may have exceeded his constitutional authority in securing this immense territory for the United States, but he showed a wise and far-seeing statesmanship in this transaction, for which he assumed the responsibility, and which now stands as the crowning achievement of his administration.

President Jefferson, although urged by his party and many friends to be again a candidate for re-election, refused the honor, and on March 4, 1809, after a continuous public service of more than forty years, laid aside the duties of President, and retired to his home at Monticello. He lived there for more than seventeen years as a private citizen, yet regarded as one of the most illustrious personages in the Republic. His advice was frequently sought and followed in political and other matters. Thus his usefulness to the Nation and the community continued through these declining years of his life.

Although President Jefferson had suffered many reverses of fortune during his public career, losing most of his property and coming in these later years to comparative poverty, having experienced family sorrows in the loss of wife and daughter, and failing in many of his cherished plans and undertakings, his noble character sustained and gave him courage, so that he was cheerful and brave-hearted to the end of life.

The illness of Mr. Jefferson was a brief one. He died at Monticello, July 4, 1826, his life-long friend, although sometimes his political opponent and rival, John Adams, dying on the same day. This date is memorable as the fiftieth anniversary of the adoption of the Declaration of Independence, in the framing of which Jefferson and Adams were both interested, Jefferson drafting the famous document and doing so much for its support. In estimating the character of Jefferson it may be truly said that a love of freedom and toleration sank deep into his nature, and to promote the cause of liberty he was willing to work with brain and hand, to endure opposition and hardships, to hold office, or, at the call of duty, relinquish honors, that his country might win in the struggle for truth and the right. A nation lives in such heroic souls as these, and, as his more enlightened countrymen of to-day pay their tributes to the hero and patriot, they think with wonder of Jefferson's abilities as student and statesman; as philanthropist, when the humanities were not encouraged as now; as founder of a university at Charlottesburg, Virginia, when education was by no means the ruling power it is to-day, and realize the security and strength of the Republic as it embodies the life-principles of such men as these, such pillars of mighty thoughts and giant deeds.

JAMES MADISON.

FOURTH PRESIDENT OF THE UNITED STATES.

JAMES MADISON.

PRESIDENT, MARCH 4, 1809 — MARCH 4, 1817.

BOYHOOD AND STUDIOUS HABITS — COLLEGE LIFE — EARLY PUBLIC SERVICES — "FATHER OF THE CONSTITUTION"— MARRIAGE AND LIFE AT MONTPELIER — SECRETARY OF STATE — PRESIDENT DURING THE WAR OF 1812 — SECOND TERM — TREATY OF PEACE — QUIET LIFE IN HIS VIRGINIAN HOME — TRANQUILITY AND USEFULNESS OF LATER YEARS — HIS DEATH — TRIBUTES TO HIS CAREER AND GREATNESS.

EACH human life, however much of individuality it may possess, owes something in the shaping of its thought and action to outward influences of condition or surroundings. What men call inherent beliefs are but the consequences of early training, of custom, or of circumstance, such important factors in the development and upbuilding of character. Born in Virginia, March 16, 1751, at a time when the State was filled with patriotic ardor, James Madison, the fourth President of the United States, was early influenced by the atmosphere of culture and intelligent thought which surrounded him. Although his parents lived in Orange County, at Montpelier, his birthplace was in King George County, where, at the time of his birth, his mother was paying a visit to some of her relations. His father, a man of wealth and distinction, owned a large estate in the region of the Blue Ridge Mountains, and was a neighbor — as persons living within a radius of fifty miles were neighbors in those days — of Thomas Jefferson, then residing at Monticello, twenty-five

miles away. Although the lad was a member of a family con-
sisting of seven children, he was never very fond of boyish
sports or out-door play, but preferred study and his books to
anything else, and under the direction of a private tutor,
applied himself diligently to the acquisition of knowledge,
becoming proficient in the ancient and some of the modern
languages. During his college life at Princeton he applied
himself so closely to his books that his health suffered in consequence, and the effects of this over-indulgence in the way of
study continued throughout his whole life, for, although never
a feeble man, his naturally strong constitution suffered a serious and enduring loss of vigor. He graduated from Princeton in 1771, and after a year more of study under the able Dr.
Witherspoon, president of the college, he returned to Virginia and began the study of law, combining it with research
and reading in the lines of philosophy and theology. His
refined home, his cultured mind, his dignified manners, his
friends and associates, all these were influences leading him
into the paths of a public service and contributing to his after
character as statesman and able defender, by word and pen, of
the principles he advocated with such ability and power.

Passing rapidly over this period of the young man's career,
a time when he was searching into theology and religion, and
grasping the truths ever after firmly held,— a time when he
was associated with Jefferson in opposing the claims of the
Church of England, in demanding and striving to establish
religious freedom in Virginia, the year 1776 marks his appearance in political affairs. He was chosen at that time delegate
to the convention which was to form the constitution for the
State of Virginia. His ability and learning were recognized
thus early in his career; his talents, as shown in the Council
of State where he served as a member under Patrick Henry
and Thomas Jefferson, the first and second governors of Vir-

ginia, made him a valued supporter of these ardent patriots. Sitting at the feet of the illustrious leaders who appreciated the worth of the young man, Madison doubtless gained much that was to help him in later years, and probably this recognition from men of admitted character and standing, assisted him to more quickly attain a well-deserved position of honor and dignity. In the year 1780 Madison became a member of the Continental Congress, serving three years with conspicuous ability, during the period which included the closing events of the Revolution, the ensuing difficulties in the government calling for a wise guidance of the new Republic.

As a delegate to the Convention of States, which adopted the Constitution, September 17, 1787, Madison labored most earnestly in debate and had more to do with moulding the form in which the provisions of the Constitution finally took shape than any other man. His work was not ended with its adoption, however; the people must accept and the states ratify it. So Madison rendered important service in its behalf, arguing its claims, explaining its features, disabusing the objections arising in the public mind, finally, in 1788, uniting with Hamilton and Jay, in writing articles, celebrated then as now, discussing and defending the merits of the Constitution. These articles in collected form were known by the name of *The Federalist*, while by these writings and his other efforts in this direction, Madison gained the well-deserved title of Father of the Constitution. Temporarily this earnest advocacy alienated him from the support of the majority of the people in his State and he was defeated as a candidate for the United States Senate, but was elected from the District in which he resided, a Representative to the lower house, taking his seat in the year 1789 and rendering important aid in organizing the new government. As a rule he did not favor the measures of Washington's administration, but sided with the opposition, becoming their acknowledged leader in the House of Representatives.

Having met with a disappointment in his affections during his early life, it was not until he was forty-three years old that Mr. Madison again lost his heart, this time to the charming Mrs. Dolly Paine Todd, a young widow who had been the reigning belle of New York and Philadelphia. His suit was successful, and they were married in the year 1794. Mrs. Madison was, in beauty of person and character, well fitted for the dignity and honors of her position. She was charming in her home life, sought after as a shining light in society, was a brilliant conversationalist, contributing not only to her husband's domestic happiness, but to the eminence and popularity of his public career.

When Madison's term in Congress expired, in 1797, he returned to his home at Montpelier, to private life, in spite of the entreaties of his friends who urged him to be a candidate for the presidency. During the administration of Mr. Adams the "Alien and Sedition Acts" were passed and aroused dissensions throughout the country, causing the Republicans and Federalists to be more bitterly antagonistic than before. Through the influence of Jefferson, Madison became actively interested in the opposition of these acts, drawing up resolutions which were carried in the Virginia Legislature, and his masterly writings during this period in favor of "strict construction," served as a text-book for his party, while some thirty years after they were used by Calhoun and others in advocating the principles of nullification, although Madison, much annoyed by such perversion, had repeatedly repudiated the idea that his arguments could be used in supporting a doctrine so opposed to his belief and judgment.

In the year 1801 Jefferson was elected President and soon appointed his friend Madison as Secretary of State, a position which he held during the eight years of Jefferson's administration. Madison was eminently fitted to fill this honorable position which called for intellectual ability, the cool and fair decisions of an able diplomat. The correspondence of Madison as Secretary of State, shows his polished style as a writer, together with his abilities as statesman and scholar. It was after this preparation that Mr. Madison was elected as President and inaugurated into his high office March 4, 1809. He followed for a time the peaceful policy of his predecessor, Thomas Jefferson, but soon became aroused by the action of Great Britain in her impressment of American sailors, so that in 1812 he signified his approval of the action of Congress in declaring war against the mother country.

In 1813 Mr. Madison was re-elected to his second term, and showed wise administrative abilities in the conduct of affairs, though he had not the bold, aggressive powers of leadership necessary to the carrying out of his own wise theories and plans. He did the best of which he was capable, but the qualities wherein he excelled, the impartial judgment, the calm reason, the dislike he had to forcing his opinions upon others, were not the attributes to make the greatest President in time of war, though they did contribute to the renown which he achieved as a statesman and constitutional authority. During the war, lasting nearly three years, the town of Washington was captured by the English, the public buildings destroyed, the President narrowly escaping capture by the British troops. None rejoiced more than Madison at the Treaty of Peace, signed at Ghent, December 24, 1814, which ended the war of 1812, made memorable by the victories won by the American navy, offsetting the numerous losses and defeats on land. The later years of Madison's administration were tranquil and pleasant ones; the country increased in prosperity, its population grew rapidly, its revenues were larger, and more than twenty-two thousand immigrants arrived in 1817, an enormous number for those early days.

Throughout the administration of Madison, the labors and influence of his cultivated wife played no small part. As a recent writer says: " She had the great gift of healthy beauty, and much clear common sense as well as quick wit; but her crowning talent was her charm of manners. She had what the French term *courtoisie de cœur*, as well as the courtesy of form also." Speaking of Mrs. Madison at her receptions in the White House, the same writer adds: " She always moved about the rooms as a lady would in her own house, and in her own bright, natural way said something to every one, especially to those shy and nervous people, which made them glow with the pleased feeling that they were welcome and made to be part of her reception."

At the close of his second term, 1817, Mr. Madison retired to his home at Montpelier, Virginia, spending his closing years quietly and happily, interested in agricultural pursuits, consulted as an authority upon political affairs, entertaining his friends and neighbors and maintaining his interest in study and education. He was once again called to act in the public service by becoming a member of the State Convention of Virginia, which met to revise its constitution in 1829. He also delivered several addresses and speeches in these later years, maintaining his reputation as a gifted writer, a logical thinker, to the close of life. His death took place June 28, 1836, when he had reached the age of eighty-five years.

The quiet, studious boy in the home at Montpelier, the courteous, gentle youth at college, the learned counsel and impartial statesman, the dignified Secretary of State, the firm yet peaceful President of the Republic, the dearly-loved husband and friend in the quiet of his declining years, these are the pictures which the life of James Madison most vividly presents. The hints of character shown in boyhood developed through middle life and age into a harmonious, rounded-out existence, marked by no bursts of genius, no wonderful ideas or startling actions. America has reason to be proud of producing a man so scholarly and tolerant, so conciliatory and judicial, so courteous a gentleman, although he had never visited the old world or hardly traveled beyond the borders of Virginia. He was criticised, perhaps justly, for his timidity, and certainly he had not the qualities of a bold leader in political opposition, yet his quiet, analytical arguments, above all, his own calmness of judgment, often convinced men and helped his cause as much as more aggressive movements might have done.

Madison's married life was very happy: he was a husband, she a wife, whose examples make domestic felicity the sublime state here on earth, and teach humanity what a true marriage may mean. The dutiful son, caring so tenderly for his mother throughout her long life, could not fail to be otherwise, and the respect for old age which ever characterized Madison was a striking attribute of his noble nature. As a writer he was wonderfully gifted; his literary style is excellent; his language and form of expression models in their special lines of composition. These documents which he carefully prepared are valuable studies for the statesman and political leaders of to-day, not only for their literary merits, but also for the products of intellect and learning which they embody. The great talents of Madison, his distinguished position, his long and honored life have given him a place forever in the pages of history; his manly attributes, his sterling virtues, his gracious disposition, his pure, unsullied character have given him a higher rank in the hearts of the American people.

JAMES MONROE.

FIFTH PRESIDENT OF THE UNITED STATES.

JAMES MONROE.

DISTINGUISHED ANCESTRY — STUDENT AND SOLDIER — COMMISSIONED AS COLONEL — IN LEGISLATURE AND COUNCIL. — DIPLOMATIC CAREER — GOVERNOR OF VIRGINIA — EMINENT POSITIONS AS SECRETARY OF WAR AND STATE — FIFTH PRESIDENT OF THE REPUBLIC — "MONROE DOCTRINE." — THE STORY OF HIS OLD AGE — A TRIBUTE TO HIS NOBLE CHARACTER.

THE most democratic of men must derive a certain amount of pleasure in tracing his ancestry to the distinguished leaders of a past age, to the honest, courageous souls, sometimes of noble name, always of noble nature, who played important parts in shaping the destinies of nations or communities. Certainly it must be admitted that biographers are prone to touch upon the family distinctions of their subject, while readers are always delighted to think of their hero as descended from a notable and historic line of ancestors. Although it is true that great men have sprung from very lowly beginnings, from obscure families of almost unknown origin, it is equally a fact that, even in democratic America, the history of some of her ablest leaders brings them into view as only sharing in the triumphs and distinguished careers of a race born to influence men and affairs. Thus it is that James Monroe, the fifth President of these United States, belonged to an honorable and somewhat influential family, one of his ancestors, Hector Monroe, being prominent among the Scottish cavaliers of the seventeenth century, an officer ardently devoted

4

to the fortunes of that ill-fated monarch, Charles I. The descendants of this Scottish cavalier were prominent among the early settlers of the New World, and the Monroe family, living in Westmoreland County, Virginia, where James was born April 28, 1758, were prosperous and well-known people. It is of interest to note the fact that four of the early Presidents of our Republic, Washington, Jefferson, Madison, and Monroe, were born and reared in the same region, lying in the vicinity of the Blue Ridge Mountains; were doubtless affected by the same influences, imbibed the common principles of patriotic zeal, and shared in a like service for their country's prosperity.

James, the subject of this sketch, was a bright, intelligent boy, a thoughtful student, yet not so devoted to his books as to neglect the sports of boyhood or the enjoyments of out-door life. After an excellent preparation in a classical school, he entered William and Mary College when he was sixteen years of age, having already learned to appreciate the value of the best possible education, as a foundation for life-work in any direction. This was an eventful time in the history of the country. The air was filled with rumors of impending war and it was with difficulty that young Monroe could properly attend to his work as a college student. At length his patriotic ardor so impelled him to take active service in defense of his country that he left college in 1776, at once going to General Washington's headquarters in New York, there taking his place as a volunteer in the ranks of the American army.

Monroe, after following the army in its retreat through New Jersey, taking part in several engagements, was wounded at the battle of Trenton, where he so distinguished himself that he was promoted, receiving a commission as captain. He accepted, a little later, a position on the staff of General Armstrong, doing creditable service in the battles of Brandywine, Germantown, and Monmouth. He was regarded with favor by General Washington, who gave him a commission as colonel, together with the authority to raise and equip a regiment of Virginia volunteers. This undertaking was for many reasons, none of them reflecting upon his ability or patriotism, however, unsuccessful, so that Colonel Monroe decided to carry out his early plan of entering the legal profession, thus ending his military career, although he volunteered, at a later period, in defense of Virginia, and stood always ready to engage in the scenes of battle, whenever his services should be required. He studied law in the office of Mr. Jefferson, then governor of Virginia, who probably did much towards forming the character of the young man, as well as directing his professional studies.

It was but a short time after Monroe began the practice of law that he was called into public life, to take part in the legislative councils of his country. He assumed the responsibilities and duties of a member of the Virginia Legislature in the year 1782, and was a little later chosen by that body as a member of the executive council. He was called to represent Virginia in the Continental Congress of 1783, taking his seat as a member of that body, in time to be a witness of the memorable scene at Annapolis, Maryland, when General Washington resigned his commission to that authority which he always recognized as a supreme power. In the debates of Congress, Colonel Monroe took part with ability and judgment, soon gaining a position of prominence and, young as he was, exerting a very considerable influence. Under a law then in force, he was ineligible for re-election, and retired from the legislature at the expiration of his term of service, in the year 1786. It was during the closing year of his membership in Congress that Monroe met Miss Kortright, whom he married, after a comparatively brief courtship, and with whom he lived happily throughout the half-century of their earthly existence.

While serving in Congress, Mr. Monroe became impressed with the inadequacy of the Articles of Confederation as a form of rule for the government of the new Republic. He deemed these articles unsuitable to the prevailing modes of thought and life among the American people, so he favored the formation of a new constitution which should augment the dignity and power of the central government. When, however, the constitution, framed in 1787, was offered for the public adoption, Monroe opposed its ratification, in the convention of Virginia, where he was a member, because he believed that it would grant too much power to the government, and for other reasons was not what the people required. In following out this course of action, based upon his best judgment, he antagonized the views of Mr. Madison, who had earnestly argued in behalf of the new constitution, and of many others among his associates and friends. The Virginia convention finally adopted the constitution as presented, Mr. Monroe finding himself in the minority. His opinions upon this matter did not seem to affect his popularity among his constituents, for, in 1789, he was elected a United States Senator by the Virginia Legislature. He actively opposed many of the leading features of Washington's administration, but that great-minded and tolerant President saw only the integrity and honest purpose of Monroe, and retained him in his confidence and friendship, notwithstanding these important differences of opinion. This is shown by Washington's act in appointing Monroe as Minister to France in 1794, in the place of Governeur Morris, recalled in accordance with the request of the French Government. Monroe, who belonged to the party sympathizing, to a large degree, with the rulers and people of France, was welcomed in that country with great rejoicings and enthusiasm. His course at Paris, however, was not in conformity with President Washington's ideas as to the strict neutrality which his administration ought to maintain, as between France and England, and in 1796 Mr. Monroe was recalled. In the year 1799, he became governor of Virginia and was twice re-elected to that office. Soon after Jefferson's accession to the presidency, he was again sent abroad in a diplomatic capacity as Envoy Extraordinary to France, there aiding Mr. Livingston, minister to that country, in his negotiations for the purchase of New Orleans and contiguous territory. Having concluded this special business, he proceeded to England, acting under a commission as minister to that country in place of Rufus King. At this time, also, his services as diplomat were called into requisition to aid in settling a controversy with Spain. This attempt was unsuccessful, as was also the chief purpose he had in view in his relations with England, namely, that of negotiating a treaty with Great Britain, which should be more favorable to the interests of the United States.

Mr. Monroe, who refused to antagonize Madison as a candidate for the presidency, was again elected governor of Virginia, in 1811, but hardly had he entered upon the duties of that office before he was invited to take the place of Secretary of State, that office having been made vacant by the retirement of Robert Smith. Mr. Monroe accepted the appointment and held the office during the remainder of Mr. Madison's administration. As Secretary of State he took a bold, decided stand against the encroachments of England, and advocated a policy which resulted in an open rupture with that country in 1812. After the capture of the capital, Mr. Monroe assumed the duties of the war department, in addition to those devolving upon him as Secretary of State, evincing much energy and ability in obtaining supplies and applying measures requisite for a vigorous prosecution of the war. His patriotism was specially shown by pledging his private credit, as subsidiary to that of the government, to provide the needful outfit and equipment for the army defending New Orleans. By this act New Orleans was successfully defended, the British army defeated, and an honorable peace was soon brought about.

Mr. Monroe was elected President in 1816, and re-elected almost unanimously four years later. His administration of the government was marked by a liberal and progressive spirit, and was generally satisfactory. Although a disciple of Jefferson and elected by the Democratic party, he yet chose a course of public action which commended him to the Federalists, while it did not take from him the support of his own party. At that time, however, party lines were well nigh obliterated, old issues had lost their bitterness, and new lines of difference had not yet been marked out. It was indeed an "era of good feeling" when the President found it comparatively easy to bring into his Cabinet prominent men representing both parties, and to pursue a course of administrative action approved by a large majority of the American people. At first he was too strict in his construction of the Constitution, as defining the powers of the general government, to favor a system of internal improvements, but finally he yielded his own scruples in this respect in order to advance the nation's welfare. His administration was distinguished by the acquisition of Florida, obtained from Spain, in 1819, by the payment of $5,000,000, the admission of five new states, the avowal and insistence of a policy relating to foreign nations, since known as the "Monroe Doctrine," under which no European interference on this continent was to be allowed, and the passage of the "Missouri Compromise," after a prolonged struggle over the admission of Missouri, during which the "era of good feeling" was disturbed by the growing hostility manifested between the Slave States and the Free States, and the strife of each section to obtain increase of power. Notwithstanding the feeling thus awakened, the country greatly prospered during the eight years of President Monroe's administration, marked by many evidences of his wise, patriotic, and statesmanlike career. After leaving the presidential office, he took up his residence at Oak Hill, Loudoun County, Virginia, where he passed the remainder of his years in an honorable retirement. His death occurred July 4, 1831, at the residence of his son-in-law, Samuel L. Goveneur, of New York, with whom he was temporarily residing as guest and visitor.

The men who founded this Republic were influenced in thought, were roused to action, by the self-same principle of patriotic devotion, impelling them to active service in behalf of their native land. With this one motive as a basis for the formation of character each of these early leaders worked out his own personality, exercising his various talents to further the prosperity of his country along individual lines of well-defined, persistent effort. President Monroe was lacking in some of the qualities which distinguished the other patriotic leaders of his time, yet he was a man of intelligent thought, of varied intellectual powers, of dignified bearing, a true patriot and an illustrious statesman. He was thoroughly reliable, an honest gentleman, conducting himself as such in all the high positions of public trust which he was called to fill. He was a true friend to those who enjoyed his confidence, was utterly unselfish, desired his country's good above all personal considerations, and was a singularly pure-minded product of the best American civilization.

JOHN QUINCY ADAMS.

SIXTH PRESIDENT OF THE UNITED STATES.

JOHN QUINCY ADAMS.

PRESIDENT MARCH 4, 1825 — MARCH 4, 1829.

CROSSING THE OCEAN — IRREGULAR EDUCATION IN EUROPE — THE YOUTHFUL
SECRETARY — RETURN HOME AND GRADUATION AT HARVARD — STUDY AND
PRACTICE OF LAW — APPOINTED BY WASHINGTON MINISTER TO THE HAGUE —
HIS MARRIAGE — IMPORTANT DIPLOMATIC SERVICES — SECRETARY OF STATE
UNDER PRESIDENT MONROE — ELECTED PRESIDENT — SEVENTEEN YEARS'
CONGRESSIONAL SERVICE — HIS DEATH AT THE CAPITOL — ILLUSTRATIONS
OF CHARACTER.

EARLY in the month of February of the year 1778, the
good ship *Boston* lay at anchor in Massachusetts Bay.
The frigate was waiting for its distinguished passenger,
America's Ambassador to France, John Adams, who, in company with his son, John Quincy, a boy of ten years, went on
board the *Boston* one stormy winter day, leaving his brave
wife and little family in the shelter of his native land, while he
devoted himself to serving his country's interests, enduring
risks and hardships, sacrificing all personal ambitions at the
call of patriotic duty. It was this lad, born in the quiet town
of Quincy, Massachusetts, July 11, 1767, separated from his
mother and childhood home at so early an age, who afterwards, in the course of events, was called to fill the honored
position of Chief Magistrate of this Republic.

Born at too late a period to take part in the Revolutionary
War, at a time when the government of the Republic had
already been founded, John Quincy Adams early acquired a
love of freedom; received as a boy lasting impressions of the

meaning of war, the principles of liberty, the resistance of oppression, and the defense of the right. He never forgot the sight he witnessed when only eight years old, the spectacle of burning Charlestown, the smoke from the battle of Bunker Hill, the sounds of war which at that time he heard. On board the *Boston*, also, there were British frigates encountered, and a prize taken, so that the boy quickly learned the importance attached to his country's welfare and the services which must be rendered in her behalf. Naturally an intelligent lad, this life of travel and intercourse with distinguished men taught him in ways not possible to the average youth, while to offset this he lost something of the advantages connected with home training and a systematic education.

When John Adams again crossed the ocean in 1779, being empowered by the President to negotiate a treaty of peace with Great Britain, John Quincy accompanied his father, traveling with him from Spain to Paris, beginning on this journey to keep a diary, as a record of daily events, a practice which he continued throughout his life. The elder Adams resided for a time in Holland, so the boy was sent to school in Amsterdam, afterwards studying for a brief period in the University of Leyden. When a youth of fifteen, he accompanied Mr. Francis Dana in his unsuccessful mission to St. Petersburg, acting in the capacity of a private secretary. After the journey back to Holland, which he took alone, he joined his father, entering the best society of The Hague and profiting by an intercourse with the diplomats there assembled. When John Adams was appointed Ambassador to the Court of St. James in 1785, his son preferred to return to America, relinquishing the brilliant life in London for the student career of an American college, as he already felt the love for his country and its institutions which afterwards impelled him in his performance of all public service. He graduated from Harvard College with honor, in July, 1787.

The young law student was admitted to the bar in 1791,
after having pursued his legal studies under Theophilus Par-
sons, of Newburyport, afterwards Chief Justice of Massachusetts. He took an interest in public affairs early in life, writing articles upon political subjects, showing very quickly the
abilities of a rising young man. In a series of articles published about this time, Mr. Adams argued in favor of the strict
neutrality which he thought it was the duty of the United States
to maintain in the war impending between France and England.
These ideas, in conformity with the thought and policy of
President Washington, doubtless influenced him in his choice
of Ambassador to The Hague, an appointment which he gave
to Adams in the year 1794. Although John Adams was Vice-
President at this time, he exercised no influence in securing the
appointment of his son, Washington acting in the matter without his counsel or even knowledge. Thus it is that we find
John Quincy Adams enjoying the confidence of Washington,
honorably identified in carrying out the foreign policy of the
United States when only twenty-seven years of age. For two
years Mr. Adams remained in Holland. At the expiration of
that time, he was appointed Minister to Portugal, but while
proceeding to undertake his duties there, he received a new
commission, changing his destination to Berlin. His father,
at that time President, felt some hesitancy in appointing him,
fearing public criticism, as personal motives might be thought
to influence the action. President Adams asked counsel in
this matter of his friend, George Washington, then retired
from public office, who replied in a letter bearing testimony to
the high esteem in which he held both father and son, one of
its clauses being as follows: " I give it as my decided opinion,
that Mr. Adams is the most valuable public character we have
abroad; and that there remains no doubt in my mind, that he
will prove himself to be the ablest of all our diplomatic corps."

Just before proceeding to the Court of Berlin, Mr. Adams, waiting in London for instructions from his government, married Miss Louisa Catherine Johnson, daughter of the American Consul in that city. Mrs. John Quincy Adams would have been a notable woman in any position; as the wife of the distinguished American statesman, she received the respectful homage to which, because of her beauty, accomplishments, and intelligence, she was entitled.

While serving in the capacity of Ambassador to Berlin Mr. Adams conducted negotiations with skillful diplomacy, concluding a commercial treaty with Prussia before he was recalled to this country by President Jefferson in the year 1801. He returned to this country with a reputation already established for a scholarly statesmanship, while, on resuming his law practice in Boston, he added to the renown already won by the judicial learning which he displayed. Soon called to public life again, he served one term in the Massachusetts Senate, afterwards, in 1803, he was elected United States Senator. Although in general sympathy with the opinions of the Federal side in politics, Mr. Adams held to more moderate political views; he separated himself almost entirely from his party in supporting the Embargo Bill, which had been recommended by President Jefferson. He was censured for this course by the Massachusetts Legislature, consequently he resigned his place in the Senate, and retired to private life.

During the three years which followed, Mr. Adams not only attended to the duties of his profession, but also ably filled the Chair of Rhetoric and Belles Lettres at Harvard College, giving lectures which were received with approbation by the students and other scholarly men. These lectures were published, attracting favorable notice in the literary as well as the social world. Mr. Adams returned to public life soon after the accession of Mr. Madison to the presidency, receiving an appointment, in 1809, as United States Minister to Russia. He soon gained the confidence of the Russian Emperor, a valuable influence of good at the time when war broke out between England and the United States, for, as a result of this confidence, Russia offered her mediation to both belligerent nations. Thus it was that, though England declined this offer of mediation, she was led to signify her willingness to deal directly with the United States, and so peace was brought about. Mr. Adams was at the head of the commission which, after six months of negotiation, came to an agreement with the English Commissioners, the treaty of peace being signed at Ghent, December 24, 1814. Shortly after this date Mr. Adams was promoted to fill the office of Minister to England, well performing the duties of this important diplomatic position until he was recalled to his native land in the year 1817 to assume the responsible place of Secretary of State under President Monroe. He acted in this capacity for eight years, helping to shape the foreign policy of Mr. Monroe's administration, and deserving credit for many of the measures which distinguished that period.

The candidates for the presidency to succeed President Monroe were Andrew Jackson, William Henry Crawford, Henry Clay, and John Quincy Adams. There was no choice made by the electoral college, so the election was by the House of Representatives, voting by states, Mr. Adams being elected as a result of the first ballot.

The administration of President Adams was decidedly unpopular, especially among the friends of General Jackson, whose increased popularity resulted in his election as President over Adams in the campaign of 1828. John Quincy Adams seems to have inherited something of the austerity, coupled with the cold manners, which characterized his father, so that his personality drew towards him few personal or party friends. The younger Adams was not an intense partisan; followed his individual thought to whatever distances it might lead away from his political party, but he was always true to his own best convictions as to his country's interests and welfare. During his administration there was great material progress throughout the country, the President being foremost to promote all national improvements.

When General Harrison was inaugurated in March of the year 1829, Mr. Adams retired to his home in Quincy, thinking to spend his remaining years on earth quietly as a country gentleman, enjoying the competency afforded him by his father's fortune in addition to his own. But Massachusetts needed his services; he was elected from his district to Congress, and kept there by repeated re-elections until the time of his death. In Congress he maintained his independent position, holding aloof from both parties to a great extent. He was scholarly, judicial, and able, possessing rare acquisitions for congressional leadership. He struggled persistently for the "right of petition," and witnessed, in 1845, the abolition of the "gag rule," restricting the right to petition Congress on the subject of slavery.

It was when the "old man eloquent" was gaining more and more of his associates' respect and love that he was stricken down, while in the Hall of Representatives, with a paralytic attack, February 21, 1848. He was carried to the Speaker's room in the Capitol, where, under the roof which had echoed with his ringing speeches in behalf of human rights, he breathed the last feeble words, so consistent with the whole tenor of his life, "This is the end of earth; I am content."

There are two or three notable pictures in the career of this distinguished patriot that come into the mind whenever his name is mentioned. One is of the youthful traveler and associate of celebrated men, early trained into the forms of cultivated society, yet never accommodating himself to the ceremonies foreign to his nature, nor assuming those graceful manners which might have been expected from his education so cosmopolitan in its surroundings.

The second picture is that of the man advanced in life, who, with blazing eyes and a heart beating so warmly in defense of what he thought was the right, stood up in the House of Representatives, making that grand speech which silenced all antagonisms, as he argued in behalf of the petition, objected to by the House, because several of its signatures were those of women.

Again another picture presents itself as the pages of history are reviewed. When, in the reorganization of the Twenty-sixth Congress, December, 1839, the disputed seats of New Jersey occasioned trouble in the choice of speaker, it was John Quincy Adams, who in response to repeated calls, rose, and made a speech advocating decisive action in the matter. When it was asked how the question should be put, as the clerk refused to act, amid tumultuous applause, Mr. Adams replied, " I will put the question myself." Mr. Wise, of Virginia, in commending this speech said, "If, when you are gathered to your fathers, I were asked to select the words which in my judgment are the best calculated to give at once the character of the man, I would inscribe upon your tomb this sentence, 'I will put the question myself.'" The world has accepted this epitaph as expressing the force of character possessed by John Quincy Adams, which showed itself, not only in that one memorable act, but in the whole course of his long and useful public career.

ANDREW JACKSON.

SEVENTH PRESIDENT OF THE UNITED STATES.

ANDREW JACKSON.

A SETTLER'S HOME — A BOY OF FOURTEEN IN THE REVOLUTIONARY WAR — PRAC-
TICES LAW IN NASHVILLE — ROMANTIC MARRIAGE — UNITED STATES SENA-
TOR — JUDGE OF THE SUPREME COURT — INDIAN CAMPAIGNS — BATTLE OF
NEW ORLEANS — PRESIDENT FOR TWO TERMS — HIS ADMINISTRATION — NUL-
LIFICATION IN SOUTH CAROLINA — RETURNS TO PRIVATE LIFE — DEATH —
HIS TRUE CHARACTER.

EVERY man owes something to his fatherland. A nation
has no favoritism to bestow; she gives to all her children the same virgin soil, out of which grow the weeds,
or the useful plant, as individuality asserts itself in the development of character. Men may be trained in lines divergent
as the poles, yet they will still possess certain characteristics
common to all their countrymen; there is a vein of similarity
running through every child of the same nationality, however it
may be concealed in the expansion of individual life. It is this
thought which is forcibly presented as the life of Andrew
Jackson is reviewed. He represents a type of the American
character, widely differing from the earlier Presidents of the
Republic, presenting a specially marked contrast to his immediate predecessor in office, John Quincy Adams. Andrew
Jackson was born amid the humblest surroundings, in a log-
cabin, of a Carolina settlement, enduring privation and want,
early thrown upon his own resources; while Adams had all
the advantages of foreign culture, together with a college
education, the influences of a refined home and intelligent

friends.   Both men inherited something in common from
their mother country, enabling them to serve her equally well,
though aided by such different resources and possessing capabilities of so opposite a nature.

The life of the seventh President of the United States began
on March 15, 1767.   His family was numbered among the
early settlers of Waxham, situated near the line which divides
North from South Carolina.   They had a hard struggle to
obtain the necessities of life, and the father, broken down by
overwork and privation, died in the year 1767.   The widow
abandoned the desolate log-cabin, and, with her two sons, was
sheltered in the family of her married sister, living near by,
until after the birth of Andrew, which occurred amid the surroundings of destitution and sorrow.   Removing at a little
later period to the home of another relative, Mrs. Jackson
worked early and late to maintain her boys in respectable circumstances.   Andrew was sent to the rough school in the settlement, where he obtained the little education which he
received.   He was not an attractive boy; one could hardly
expect him to be, subjected as he was to rough usage, and the
influences which surrounded that hard frontier life.   He was
undisciplined, quick to resent a supposed injury, passionate in
speech and action, showing, however, one redeeming virtue in
his love for the mother who sought in her humble way for his
welfare, laying the foundation of that filial devotion and respect, which continued until her death, and gave rise, probably,
to his well-known chivalric opinions in regard to woman.

The courageous lad of fourteen years bore a slight part
in the Revolution, fighting gallantly the Tories and troops
under General Tarleton, who had invaded the Carolinas.   His
brother Hugh, when only eighteen years old, had lost his life
at the battle of Stono; while Robert and Andrew Jackson,
taken prisoners by a party of dragoons in 1781, suffered cruel

treatment from their captors, the effects of which caused the death of Robert, while Andrew's life was only saved by the extraordinary strength of his constitution. After his recovery he studied law at Salisbury, North Carolina, being admitted to the bar, and beginning a law practice in Nashville, Tennessee, where he afterwards made his home. In this vicinity, then on the borders of civilization, he made many friends, and gained reputation as a lawyer. Here he met Mrs. Rachel Robards, whom he married in the year 1791, both parties supposing that her divorce from Louis Robards had been granted. Through some technicality it was not legal, and they were re-married in the year 1794. Mr. Jackson was always sensitive on this subject, thinking so highly of his wife that he resented any imputation upon her character. Their married life was exceedingly happy, though Mrs. Jackson's position was made painful at times, and her husband annoyed, by their union becoming a cause for public discussion and scandal.

Mr. Jackson began his public career in 1797, when he was appointed to fill a vacancy in the United States Senate, where he served during the winter session of 1797–8. It was at this time, in the year 1798, that he was elected Judge of the Supreme Court of Tennessee, holding this position for a period of six years. During the next seven or eight years we find Judge Jackson enjoying a quiet home-life in his residence, the "Hermitage," situated near Nashville. Here he found opportunities to engage in business transactions, combining them with his pursuit of farming. It was during this time that he became involved in many disputes by reason of his quick temper and hasty judgment in the difficulties arising from the conditions of society as it then existed. He fought several duels, mortally wounding his antagonist, Charles Dickenson, in one of them, and receiving severe injuries himself in another encounter.

When the War of 1812 broke out, General Jackson, who had already acquired some military skill and experience, offered his services to President Madison, pledging himself to raise a supporting force of twenty-five hundred volunteers. His offer was accepted; he became a skillful military leader, manifesting early in the campaign those qualities of endurance, strength, and will power, which earned for him the suggestive title of "Old Hickory." His attributes made him a specially successful commander in the campaigns against the Indians — the powerful Creek and other tribes, who, under their famous chief, Tecumseh, had been won over as British allies. Jackson's troops gained decisive victories, so that the power of these formidable tribes was forever broken.

General Jackson was appointed major-general in the regular army of the United States, May 31, 1814, and was immediately ordered to the defense of New Orleans, where the British were then concentrating their forces. Acting under his new commission, Jackson's first move was one of peace. He succeeded in making a treaty with the Indians of Alabama and vicinity, so that they should not enter into an alliance with the enemy. It was as early as November of the year 1814, that he captured Pensacola, used by the British as a base of operations, and only a few months later, January 8, 1815, he fought and won the memorable battle of New Orleans. The defeat of the well-disciplined English troops, whose experienced commander, General Pakenham, was killed on the field of battle, was a signal victory for Jackson, made more apparent when, very quickly after the battle, the British were forced to evacuate New Orleans. The country was wild in its rejoicings over this event, and General Jackson became the Nation's hero.

Idleness was not possible to General Jackson, so in the year 1818–19 he was active in the Seminole War, fighting the

Indians and entering upon Spanish territory, an act for which he was much criticised. The purchase of Florida, however, put an end to the diplomatic questions suggested by the course of this impulsive commander. In the year 1821 he was appointed governor of Florida, but soon after resigned this office, not approving of the powers with which he was vested.

Again, General Jackson took his seat in the United States Senate, in 1823. The year following he was a candidate for the presidency, receiving the largest number of votes from the electoral college. There was, however, no choice, and the House of Representatives elected John Quincy Adams, February 9, 1825. General Jackson firmly believed this to be the result of collusion between Henry Clay, one of the candidates, and Mr. Adams; this thought was confirmed by the fact that Mr. Clay afterwards held office in the Cabinet of President Adams. General Jackson wrote and said many harsh, bitter words at this time, his hasty judgment leading him to utterances characteristic of his impetuous temperament — utterances made with little regard for the consequences which might ensue. One of his letters, concerning the matter, contains the following sentence: "I have been informed that Mr. Clay has been offered the office of Secretary of State, and that he will accept it; so you see the Judas of the West has closed the contract and will receive the thirty pieces of silver."

In the fall of 1825 General Jackson resigned his seat in the Senate of the United States, returning to his home near Nashville, where he lived as a private citizen until he was elected to the presidency in 1828. The political campaign of that year was carried on in a bitterly personal manner. General Jackson was assailed with unsparing severity, but triumphantly elected, the vote in the electoral college being one hundred and seventy-eight for him, against seventy-eight for Mr. Adams. In 1832 he was re-elected by a large majority over

Henry Clay, his chief competitor for the place, and served until March 4, 1837 — eight years in all.

The administration of General Jackson, extending over a period when political strife was most violent, was of a notable character in many respects. It was characterized by some important acts which met with popular favor. The general conduct of foreign affairs was commended, and measures, such as the removal of Indian tribes to the more distant territories, and the settlement of the French spoliation claims, were received with a good degree of public approval. Other measures, however, were unsparingly denounced by one party, although enthusiastically commended by the other. Thus it was in regard to his course respecting the establishment and rechartering of the United States Bank, and other matters relating to the financial policy, while much the same divided judgment was passed by the people on his appointments to and removals from office.

President Jackson's prompt resistance of nullification, when South Carolina in 1832 proposed to withdraw from the Union, merits special recognition. He declared the United States to be a Nation, and that no state had the right to secede from the Union, and sent General Scott to South Carolina with troops and vessels of war to repress any movement of secession. His firmness and patriotism thus manifested soon brought about acquiescence to the law on the part of the dissatisfied people of South Carolina, and the danger that had appeared so threatening, was, for a time, averted. Better now than then can the American people appreciate the bold stand taken by President Jackson in this matter, and the emphasis which he put upon the words, "The Union, it must and shall be preserved."

When public opinion puts an estimate upon character it sometimes seems that many noble qualities are left entirely out of account, just because they lead to actions not in harmony with the prevailing thought. History presents a broader view with the progress of civilization, and men like Andrew Jackson are more wisely judged, as their petty differences of opinion, their minor faults, their lack of culture or attainments sink into oblivion, while the enduring record of the positive attributes which made their influence felt upon the destiny of the Nation, grows brighter with each succeeding year.

It is good for us to remember Andrew Jackson for his honesty of purpose and life, the integrity of his nature, which betrayed itself amid the rough surroundings of the new world settlers, in the camp of the American Army, as well as during his eight years of service as the honored President of the United States. That the rough soldier, the stern leader, the passionate opponent, had yet another, more gentle side to his nature, those of his contemporaries who knew him best bore testimony. He was never too busy to entertain or watch over a little child, never too careless of another's suffering to leave a beggar in distress, never willing to listen to any adverse criticism of a woman, while he always reverenced the memory of his devoted mother, and gave to his wife the whole affection of his noble, warm heart. Quick to resent an injury, he would turn aside from any pursuit in order to confer a favor upon one of his many friends whom his personal magnetism drew towards him in an enduring association. This is a type of manhood that America does well to honor in these days when the simple republican virtues are sometimes forgotten as men celebrate the scholar and the distinguished statesman.

MARTIN VAN BUREN.

EIGHTH PRESIDENT OF THE UNITED STATES.

MARTIN VAN BUREN.

INFLUENCE OF PARENTS — ACADEMY AT KINDERHOOK — INCREASING LAW PRAC-
TICE — IN THE SENATE — GOVERNOR OF NEW YORK — EFFICIENT HELPFUL-
NESS IN THE ELECTION OF JACKSON — SECRETARY OF STATE — MINISTER TO
THE COURT OF ST. JAMES — REJECTION BY THE SENATE. — ELECTED VICE-
PRESIDENT — ATTAINS THE PRESIDENCY — HIS ADMINISTRATIVE COURSE —
PLEASANT OLD AGE — ELEMENTS OF A JUST POPULARITY.

IN the story of the Presidents of the United States there
occur several chapters which record fewer stirring events
or memorable issues than are found in the other, perhaps
more interesting pages. These lives, less notable in their
attainments, influence, however, the progress of nations, just
as the constant dropping of a tiny, noiseless stream eventually
wears away the rock which the volcanic eruption had left un-
touched in its path of destruction. So a nation needs the
quiet lives to weave into its history; the men of earnest convictions and wise statesmanship who impress their individuality
upon epochs, just as much as it requires its dashing, military
heroes, who appeal more strongly to the admiration of the general public. Thus the life of Martin Van Buren, eighth President of this Republic, affords little material for the graphic
writer to indulge in romantic, sensational biography, if he seeks
truthfully to depict the career of one who most distinguished
himself in intellectual and political achievements.

Mr. Van Buren, Martin's father, kept the village tavern in
the old town of Kinderhook, on the banks of the Hudson

River, and made that inn a popular resort of the traveler because of the hearty good-humor displayed by the genial proprietor, whose ancestors were numbered among the earliest settlers of the region, the well-to-do families from Holland who made their homes on the shores of that noble stream. The mother of the future President was also of Dutch origin, having an intelligent, well-trained mind — a superior woman for those early times. The boy, Martin, born December 5, 1782, was educated amid these influences, and inherited, doubtless, a love for mental acquirements, as well as that imperturbable good humor which characterized the father and descended to the son, although, perhaps, in a more refined form. There was a basis of character inherited, good habits early inculcated, and all liking for study encouraged, so that Martin Van Buren early developed a quick perception, a ready wit, scholarly tendencies, and a genial, pleasant manner. He attended the academy of Kinderhook, making such rapid progress while there that he was fitted to enter college, in an advanced class, at an unusually early age. He decided not to do this, however, but devote himself entirely to his law studies and enter upon the profession which he had chosen. At first he studied in a law office at Kinderhook; afterwards he went to New York City, where he continued his student life under the direction of William P. Van Ness, until the year 1803, when he returned to his native town, beginning there his practice in the legal profession.

Although as a lawyer Mr. Van Buren was energetic, prompt, and suave, soon gaining the reputation as an able advocate which he highly prized, he was a natural politician, having political instincts and likings from the first. The tavern-keeper of Kinderhook had been an ardent Republican, so that the son imbibed a strong attachment to Jefferson, to the political principles and policy of that great leader, together with the feeling that every true man must hold opinions and be actively interested in whatever pertains to the good of his country. The intelligent knowledge thus acquired upon the great questions of the day, while not interfering with the pursuits of his profession, prepared him for the career of public service which he was soon destined to undertake.

His growing reputation as a lawyer led him to seek larger opportunities for the use of his talents, so he removed, in the year 1809, to Hudson, the shire-town of his county. In this year he had assumed the responsibilities of a married man, his talented wife contributing much to his happiness during the twelve years longer allotted her on earth. Her death, of consumption, after this comparatively brief period of married life, was a great blow to Mr. Van Buren, and the unusual buoyancy of his earlier nature failed to entirely reassert itself. During the period of his life in Hudson, certainly a happy time for the young husband and successful lawyer, Mr. Van Buren won many friends, attracted to him by his talents, his intellectual abilities, his courteous, affable manners.

In 1812 his public career may be said to have had its beginning in an election to the State Senate. He was appointed Attorney-General in 1815, soon after moving his residence to Albany, a more central location for the performance of the duties incident to that honorable position. While undertaking these services of public trust, Mr. Van Buren was actively interested in political affairs, exerting upon them a somewhat powerful influence. He was not a strict adherent to party, and received, in consequence, the accusation of inconstancy. He was, however, always true to his ardent democratic principles, which sometimes carried him away from his party associates, and what appeared to be the popular feeling. Thus he warmly favored "restricted suffrage," maintaining that, while the privilege of voting should be open for the acquirement of every citizen, there ought, however, to be pre-requisite qualities of intelligence, morality, and the possession of, at least, a small amount of property. A division of the Democratic party occurred in 1818, and Mr. Van Buren became a leader of the majority section, often designated as the " Albany Regency," which was a controlling force in New York politics for a quarter of a century.

When, in the year 1821, Mr. Van Buren was elected United States Senator, his abilities as a statesman brought him speedy recognition among the foremost leaders of political affairs. He was unrelenting in opposition to the administration, in favor of " state rights," as antagonistic to the federal views entertained by President Adams. Mr. Van Buren showed himself a wise legislator, possessed of a sound judicial mind, throughout his services in the Senate, being re-elected to that body in 1827. He resigned his seat soon after, in the year 1828, to assume his duties as governor of New York, having been elected to fill that responsible position.

In the presidential contest of 1828, the name of Van Buren had prominent place. He was influential in forming and carrying out plans to defeat President Adams, giving all the force of his attainments and talents to aid in the election of General Jackson. None were more instrumental in pressing the claims of "Old Hickory," as opposed to the so-called " effeminate " John Quincy Adams, than Mr. Van Buren; none were able to render more intelligent, well-defined assistance. General Jackson, appreciating the value of these services, invited his warm adherent to accept the position of Secretary of State.

During the administration of President Jackson the powerful influence of Mr. Van Buren made itself felt. The Secretary of State was affable to friend and foe alike, capable of quickly grasping the bearings of any measure, or understanding any situation of affairs, so that his services were of great value to the government. His extraordinary talents and energy displayed at this time, made evident his fitness for the office of President, and the idea of his candidacy became probable. Mr. Jackson, as a matter of course, urged the claims of his friend Van Buren, who had so aroused, however, the enmity of Mr. Calhoun and others, that when he was appointed by the President in 1831, Minister to England, the Senate refused to ratify the nomination. Before this Mr. Van Buren had proceeded to England and had been received there with much enthusiasm. After his rejection he returned to his native land and became a candidate for the office of Vice-President, to which office he was elected at the time President Jackson was chosen for a second term. Thus he was soon called to preside over the Senate which had refused to confirm his appointment as Minister to England.

In 1836 Mr. Van Buren received the Democratic nomination for President, and was elected by a considerable majority. His inauguration, on the 4th of March, 1837, specially brilliant in its various features, was witnessed by an immense concourse of people. His inaugural address, which gave general satisfaction, was particularly pleasing to the friends of the retiring President, as it indicated the purpose of Mr. Van Buren to continue the line of policy marked out by his immediate predecessor. The whole country had confidence in the conspicuous abilities of President Van Buren, whose experience and acquisitions made him so eminently fitted for the duties he was called to discharge. But times of trial and peril were at hand, for soon there swept over the land a financial storm of unprecedented severity. There was a revulsion of national prosperity, and a dark and threatening condition of affairs. Foreign complications, Indian wars, the growing excitement in regard to the slavery question, added to the depression of business, the suspension of specie payments by the banks, and the clamors of the extremely poor then out of employment, created a feeling of dismay throughout the country. President Van Buren, called to fill the presidential office at a time beset by so many and such great difficulties, was unable to make his administration fruitful in the ways he desired. He was a candidate for re-election; but public sentiment grew strong against him, and his rival, William Henry Harrison, was chosen in the earnest campaign of 1840. Four years later the many friends of Mr. Van Buren pressed his name upon the Democratic nominating convention, but Mr. Polk bore off the honor. In 1848 the "Free-Soil" party placed him in nomination, and he received a considerable popular support in the Northern States. His life was that of a private citizen, however, from the time of his retirement from the presidency, but not by any means unduly limited or unpleasant. He died at Lindenwald, July 24, 1862.

While serving in the capacity of Minister to the Court of St. James, Mr. Van Buren was presented with a silver gilt dessert service, which was afterwards used in administering the hospitality of the White House. This President of the Republic, was often criticised because of his liking for luxurious appointments, and his well-known fondness for the refinements of cultured society. One of the men whom he frequently entertained at the Executive Mansion, joined in the attacks, laying great stress in his speeches against the President, upon the "gold spoons." Some one asked Mr. Van Buren if he really used, as had been alleged by the speaker, "gold spoons." "He ought to know," was the answer, "for he has often had them in his mouth."

Another incident, connected with Mr. Van Buren's Ministry to England, illustrates his calm, urbane bearing, which no calamity, reverse of fortune, or unexpected defeat, could change.

When the news reached him that the United States Senate had refused to ratify his appointment, he was enjoying the social pleasures of a large gathering in one of the prominent London homes. He showed no traces of the disappointment he must have felt at such a proof of enmity, or at least disapproval of his political views, but moved through the rooms with his usual gracious manner, his friendly words for all, his tact in selecting topics of conversation, always betraying his wonted self-possession.

Popularity is gained when one assumes or feels an interest in the affairs of all human beings. Mr. Van Buren had that suave manner, as he listened to the most uninteresting details, that spoke of sympathy in whatever was being said, so that each man felt himself honored by personal regard and concern. Another element entered into the popularity which distinguished this illustrious man: it was that trait of joyousness which, descending from the genial tavern-keeper of Kinderhook to his eldest born, clung to his life throughout all its changing scenes of joy or sorrow. The world always admires this happy nature, one of heaven's greatest gifts. As a modern poet truly writes:

> "Laugh, and the world laughs with you,
> Weep, and you weep alone."

There is much that is agreeable to linger over in a contemplation of this statesman who occupied the presidential chair; but it must not be forgotten that these outward gifts which made charming a personality, had a foundation of upright character, good habits, a pure life, an active intelligence, and talents of a high order. Without this basis of real worth, President Van Buren would never have occupied the high office as President, or commanded the respect which his name inspires.

WILLIAM HENRY HARRISON.

NINTH PRESIDENT OF THE UNITED STATES.

WILLIAM HENRY HARRISON.

INFLUENTIAL FATHER — COLLEGE LIFE AND MEDICAL STUDIES — SUCCESSIVE PRO-
MOTIONS IN THE UNITED STATES ARMY — PRIVATE LIFE — SERVICES IN CON-
GRESS — EFFICIENT GOVERNOR OF INDIANA — VICTORIES IN THE BATTLES OF
TIPPECANOE AND THE THAMES — DEFEAT AS PRESIDENTIAL CANDIDATE —
ELECTION IN 1840 — BRILLIANT INAUGURATION — DEATH OF THE PRESIDENT
AFTER AN ADMINISTRATION OF ONE MONTH — HIS PRINCIPLES AND INFLUENCE
UPON NATIONAL AFFAIRS.

THE State of Virginia has often formed a picturesque background for important events in the history of the American
nation. The reader of colonial records quickly learns to
associate this region with some of the most striking episodes
connected with the progress of this republic, while the truth
becomes apparent that many of the scenes connected with the
founding of the nation were laid among the Blue Ridge
Mountains or in the fertile valleys of Virginia. The subject
of this sketch, William Henry Harrison, although elected from
Ohio to fill the office of ninth President of the United States,
was born at Berkeley, Charles County, in Virginia, February
9, 1773. His father was one of the group of intelligent and
thoughtful men who were leaders in the patriotic struggles of
those early days; men distinguished for ability and culture,
who were prominent in the best society of Virginia at that
period. To this little circle, so influential in revolutionary
times, belonged General Washington, with whom Benjamin
Harrison enjoyed a confidential friendship. The elder Mr.
Harrison was Governor of Virginia for several terms, and his

signature was affixed to the Declaration of Independence. Thus the boy, William Henry, inherited a love for country and was early taught in the principles which ever afterwards were inseparable from his nature.

The residence of the Harrison family was a Virginia homestead, whose interior was brightened by all the evidences of a refined taste. There was the good cooking and skillful management of the numerous servants that prevailed in the best Virginia households of that day, while the exercise of a generous hospitality made the group, gathered about the blazing back logs, always a large one. William Henry Harrison was a favorite among his young associates as well as among his teachers and the older family friends. He had, as a boy, an active, enquiring mind, which gave him a fondness for books and a desire for wide information concerning men and things. He had acquired the basis of a thorough education when he entered Hampden Sidney College, where he devoted himself closely to his studies, graduating therefrom when nineteen years old. During the time of his college life his father had died, so the young man, thrown somewhat upon his own responsibilities, decided to go to Philadelphia, where he could pursue to best advantage the study of medicine. Several of his father's friends took an interest in the youthful medical student, among them his instructor, Dr. Rush, who had been an associate of the elder Harrison in signing the Declaration of Independence.

At this time, during the Presidency of Washington, the Indians on the frontier were committing the greatest outrages, and frightening by their depredations the settlers throughout the northwestern territory. These Indian tribes were powerful because of numbers and the abundant supplies and munitions of war furnished them by the British provincial officials. Young Harrison felt the patriotic ardor running through his veins as he learned of one and another of the atrocities which had been committed along the frontier, so that he abandoned his medical studies and gladly accepted the commission of ensign offered him by President Washington, who was then engaged in organizing an army against these hostile tribes. Harrison soon reported for duty to the officer in command, General St. Clair, at Fort Washington, on the Ohio River, and was at once actively engaged in the fortunes of the campaign. He speedily developed the traits of a good soldier, showed physical endurance unlooked for in so slight a frame, and won renown for courage and military skill unusual in so young a man. He received special commendation from General St. Clair, who recognized the soldierly characteristics of the youthful ensign. It was thus early in his military career that Mr. Harrison took a strong position in favor of the principles of temperance, adopting for himself the rule of total abstinence from all strong drink, a habit which he maintained to the end of his life. It was no easy matter for a young man to keep from drinking in those days of army service, when intemperance was the rule among the soldiers, and temptations were offered on every side; but Mr. Harrison was true to his own convictions of right, and could not be turned aside by any allurement which might be offered.

The services of this faithful soldier merited and soon received recognition by a promotion in the army, and, under General Wayne, Lieutenant Harrison fought efficiently in the bloody battles which followed one another during the Indian warfare. As aide-de-camp to General Wayne, he gave proof of courage, coolness and military skill, as displayed on the field of battle. He was again promoted in 1797 to the rank of captain, and it was about this time that he became interested in and married the daughter of one of the earliest settlers on the banks of the Maumee River.

Captain Harrison resigned his commission in the army in 1797, and was appointed secretary of the northwest territory, rendering important services to the people of that newly-organized district, who elected him, in 1799, to represent them as delegate in Congress. When, in 1801, the northwest territory was divided, Mr. Harrison was appointed governor of the section organized under the name of Indiana, which then included the present States of Indiana, Wisconsin and Illinois. For a period of twelve years Governor Harrison discharged the duties of his office with notable ability and zeal. He was specially successful in his treatment of the Indians, his campaign on the frontier having given him valuable knowledge on the subject of the methods and habits of savage life. He was able to obtain for his Government vast areas of land, about sixty millions of acres, ceded in the various important treaties which he concluded with the Indians. When, in 1811, hostilities again broke out, Captain Harrison took command of the troops and was eminently successful in the memorable battle of Tippecanoe, where his army gained a signal victory over the Indians who attacked them in greatly superior forces. After this military success he was commissioned by President Madison, in 1813, as Major-General and Commander of the Northwestern Army. Again he conducted his troops to victory, winning the battle of the Thames over the British forces and their savage allies, Tecumseh, the great Indian warrior, being killed during the encounter.

In the year 1816, General Harrison was elected to Congress as Representative from the State of Ohio. He was known as an able, active, influential member; his speeches were effective and logical, while his energy gave him a well-deserved reputation for diligence in the conduct of those affairs that claimed his official attention. While in Congress he supported the resolutions censuring General Jackson for his course in the Seminole war. This somewhat reckless military leader had pursued his own policy with but little regard for law or courts, and, in consequence of his action in the matter, he was censured by many persons in the expression of public opinion. General Harrison, in approving of the resolutions, paid a high tribute to General Jackson's gallantry, at the same time giving utterance to his opinion that the action of the famous military commander in disregarding civil laws ought to be disapproved.

In the year 1824 General Harrison served as one of the Presidential Electors from Ohio, casting his vote for Henry Clay, and that same year he was elected United States Senaator. It was four years later, in 1828, when he was appointed Minister to the Republic of Columbia by President John Quincy Adams. Only for a brief period was he continued in this diplomatic station, for he was recalled soon after the inauguration of President Jackson. While it may not be affirmed that this action of the newly elected President was altogether due to a feeling aroused by Harrison's support in Congress of the resolutions censuring General Jackson it is a fact that the friendly relations of the two men were never quite the same after the incident, and it seems but natural that something of personal feeling should have entered into the quick, positive call to return which President Jackson issued.

After this period of public service General Harrison returned to his comfortable home at North Bend, Ohio, where he passed a few years in the quiet pursuits which he enjoyed so much, indulging in the pleasant duties of a farmer and country gentleman. But his abilities as statesman and patriot were too generally known to allow of a private life, so that in 1836 he became candidate of the Whig party for the Presidency. He ran against Martin Van Buren, who was successful in the contest, but in 1840 Mr. Harrison was elected over the same candidate by an overwhelming majority. The canvass was a memorable one. The candidate of the Whig party was from Ohio, then a region of the Far West, and the log cabin, which became the emblem of his party, signified the prevailing thought concerning Western civilization. The campaign was most lively. With General Harrison was associated, as candidate for Vice-President, John Tyler of Virginia, so the political songs rang with the refrain of "Tippecanoe and Tyler, too," while the hard cider, the appropriate beverage, was drank enthusiastically to the success of the "hero of Tippecanoe."

The inauguration of President Harrison was a brilliant pageant, and was witnessed by immense throngs of the American people. The inaugural address of the President was permeated with that spirit of moderation which ruled his entire life, which controlled his actions, and which he desired his countrymen to exercise in the administration of the nation's affairs. Judging by his former attainments and his successful statesmanship, this policy would have been carried out by President Harrison in a manner to reflect honor upon himself as upon his beloved country; but this great and good man did not long live to enjoy the exalted position to which he was called. It was only a month after his inauguration that the death of President Harrison occurred; the echoes of the animated campaign and the exultant chorus of the triumphant party still sounded through the country, and the Whigs' rejoicing over a long-deferred victory was turned into mourning, not only for the able head of their party, but for the political situation sure to ensue. The death of President Harrison, April 4, 1841, was a great blow to the American nation, and his funeral awakened intense interest throughout the country, following, as it did, so soon after the imposing ceremonies connected with his inauguration.

There was a simple dignity in the character and life of President Harrison that endears his memory to every true heart wherever virtue and honest worth are acknowledged as sovereign factors in the elevation of humanity to the achievement of its highest ideals. America comes more and more to realize what great men have been a part of her history, what a debt of gratitude she owes to those who, in differing degrees, have rendered such service to establish her upon the solid foundation which to-day she occupies. These men who have stood for something in their day, compare favorably with the leaders and statesmen of other lands and times; viewed from an impartial position each has played well his part in the drama of America's establishment. The different talents, the varied acquirements have been used to make the Nation what it is, and, though men do not judge alike to-day or ever, they are more willing in this nineteenth century, as it seems, to value whatever is good, whatever makes for the prosperity of a people, even though the qualities displayed may not be in accordance with their own thought or judgment. So the just estimate of President Harrison makes prominent those principles of moderation, that temperance in all things, that well-balanced mind, those qualities of a successful military leader which were sufficient to distinguish this man above his fellows and render him capable of valuable service in behalf of his country's advancement. His was a consistent, manly career, a life overflowing with benevolence and justice towards all, a respect for the rights of every human being, however degraded its condition. He was American to the centre of his personality; rejoiced in all her prosperity, advocating no reckless measures while he advised that moderation which the impetuous sons of the new Republic were sometimes slow to heed. Such men as William Henry Harrison leave better records for future generations to admire than the more brilliant heroes of popular fancy, whose reputation, easily gained, is as easily forgotten in the progress of time.

JOHN TYLER.

TENTH PRESIDENT OF THE UNITED STATES.

JOHN TYLER.

FAVORED SURROUNDINGS — AT COLLEGE AND STUDENT IN HIS FATHER'S LAW
OFFICE — INFLUENTIAL MEMBER OF CONGRESS — SENT TO THE SENATE —
REFUSED TO OBEY STATE INSTRUCTIONS — RESIGNED HIS OFFICE IN CONSE-
QUENCE — VICE-PRESIDENT — PRESIDENT BY REASON OF GENERAL HARRISON'S
DEATH — UNSUCCESSFUL ADMINISTRATION — RETIREMENT FROM OFFICE —
CONNECTED WITH THE CIVIL WAR — CLOSING DAYS — A CHARACTER FULL
OF FAULTS, YET POSSESSING MANY REDEEMING VIRTUES.

IT is good for the American people to remember that their
leaders have frequently been men of lowly origin, that the
log cabin fitly represents the humble birth-place of some
heroic ones destined to fill highest offices and win their countrymen's respectful homage. This truth has been so much dwelt
upon that many doubt the genius of a man, unless his early surroundings were those of homespun inheritance, if not of actual
poverty. While paying all honor to any who have made for
themselves a name, coming from obscurity into the full light
of a national reputation, there is much to commemorate in
other prominent lives which have been developed by the
influences of a cultured home, surrounded by the advantages
of wealth and refinement. Some of the presidents of the United
States were thus "born to the purple," tracing their ancestry
to distinguished men, and belonging to families of high social
position. One of these favored ones was John Tyler, born
March 29, 1790, at Greenway, in Charles City, County of
Virginia.

The tenth Chief Magistrate of the nation was a precocious lad, devoting himself so assiduously to his studies that he entered William and Mary College well prepared, at an early age, graduating from that institution when but seventeen years old. He studied law for a time under Edmund Randolph, and afterwards with his father, both of whom were distinguished advocates, well known and highly esteemed throughout Virginia. He rapidly acquired distinction in the profession, and also gained a reputation for his knowledge of political matters, so that when he had but just attained his majority he was elected a member of the Virginia House of Delegates. Mr. Tyler, in December of the year 1811, took his seat in the legislature, where his abilities as a ready debater and eloquent speaker were quickly recognized. He served in this body for five successive years to the satisfaction of his constituents, who retained him in his seat by large majorities at each election.

The military services of Mr. Tyler were not of great importance, although, at the time when British forces were threatening Norfolk and Richmond, he raised a company of soldiers, of which he was placed in command, and with which he subsequently served in the Fifty-Second Regiment, stationed at Williamsburg.

When but twenty-six years old, in 1816, Mr. Tyler was elected to Congress, soon becoming conspicuous for his skill in debate, as well as for his familiarity with the important questions discussed. He won distinction during his several terms of service; he was an intense worker, applied himself diligently to master the subjects of legislation, that he might best discharge the duties which devolved upon him. By close attention to official labors his health became affected, forcing him to resign his place in Congress. He returned to his home in Charles City County, and, rapidly regaining his usual health, entered with renewed ardor upon the practice of his profession. Soon after he again accepted an election to the legislature, exerting in that body a most pronounced influence.

Mr. Tyler was elected Governor of Virginia in 1825, and re-elected the following year, almost unanimously. His administration of this important office was generally acceptable. He showed rare skill in composing sectional differences and assuaging the bitterness of party animosity, while he sought to stimulate the growth and development of his native state. At this time, when his popularity was greatest, he was elected to the United States Senate, succeeding Mr. John Randolph, the regular candidate of the Democratic party for re-election. Governor Tyler's victory, under these circumstances, was indeed a proof of the general esteem in which he was then held by the people of Virginia.

On the third of December, 1827, Mr. Tyler assumed the duties of Senator, at once allying himself with the opposers of President Adams' administration, notwithstanding the support he had received in the Virginia Legislature from its friends. He was a strict constructionist of the Constitution, disposed to limit the powers of the general government, and to sustain the doctrine of state rights. He voted against the tariff bill of 1828, and most of the measures for internal improvements which came under consideration about this time. When General Jackson succeeded to the presidency, Senator Tyler gave the new administration his support, although often pursuing an independent, not to say erratic course. He was in sympathy with Mr. Calhoun and the nullifiers of South Carolina, justifying their course on the extreme ground of state rights, while he was antagonistic to the efficient and patriotic course of President Jackson in seeking to compel the people of South Carolina to obey the laws. He gave vigorous opposition to the force bill, designed to provide for the collection of the revenue in the disaffected region, and vesting extraordinary powers in the President. At a later period, however, he used his influence in favor of the compromise and pacification measures introduced into the Senate by his personal friend, Mr. Clay.

Senator Tyler was re-elected to the Senate for six years, dating from March 4, 1833. Though nominally identified with, and owing his election to the Democratic party, he severed himself from such party affiliation by voting to sustain the resolutions introduced by Mr. Clay in 1834, censuring President Jackson for the removal of the public deposits, holding that he had exceeded his rightful authority in so doing. The Virginia legislature instructed the senators from that State, in February 1836, to vote in favor of expunging from the Senate journal the resolutions censuring President Jackson. Senator Tyler refused to obey these instructions, but held that it was not right for him to retain his seat after so refusing; therefore, he resigned his senatorship, three years only of his term having expired. His conduct in this matter was generally commended and he lost nothing of reputation by making his action in this respect conform with his previous record.

After his retirement to private life, in February, 1836, he again resumed the practice of law in Williamsburg, where he had removed his family two or three years previously. In the presidential campaign of 1836, the name of Mr. Tyler was associated with that of General Harrison on the ticket supported by the Whig party in some of the states; but Maryland was the only State which voted for Harrison that also gave its electoral vote to Mr. Tyler for Vice-President. He received, however, other votes from the state rights party of the South and West, which opposed Mr. Van Buren, so that in all he obtained forty-seven electoral votes for the office named.

At a convention of the Whig party held in 1839 at Harris-

burg, Pennsylvania, to nominate candidates for President and
Vice-President, Mr. Tyler, delegate from Virginia, zealously
supported Mr. Clay for the first place. General Harrison,
however, was nominated; then, as a sort of propitiation to the
friends of the defeated candidate, Mr. Tyler was selected as
candidate for the office of Vice-President. This position was
not thought to be specially important, no President having
died in office; the idea of Mr. Tyler's ever succeeding to the
presidency was not taken into account. Had it been, the choice
of the convention would probably have fallen on some one
more thoroughly committed to the policy of the Whig party,
one on whom a greater confidence could be placed for his reli-
ability.

The exciting campaign of 1840 has elsewhere been referred
to; it is sufficient in this connection to state that it resulted in
the triumphant election of General Harrison as President and
Mr. Tyler as Vice-President. President Harrison died one
month after his inauguration; Mr. Tyler, in accordance with
the provisions of the constitution, succeeded to the presidency, April 4, 1841. Two days later he took the oath of
office as President and entered upon the responsible duties of
that position. His course during the three years and eleven
months of his presidential service greatly disappointed the
political leaders of the country and almost completely estranged
him from his former friends. It has well been said of him that
"he lost the respect of the party by which he was elected
without gaining that of their political opponents." He vetoed
various measures supported by the party to which he owed his
election and for the most part declined to act with the majority in Congress. His successive vetoes of bills to incorporate
a national bank caused great indignation. He was accused of
bad faith, of working for a re-nomination which he thought he
might secure from the opposition, with whom he was most in

sympathy, though he was not much liked or greatly trusted by them. His administration was characterized by several important acts and measures, one of them being the settlement of the difficulties with Great Britain, by the adjustment of the northeastern boundary between Canada and the United States. Another important negotiation was the treaty with China, while the annexation of the republic of Texas awakened bitter opposition, partly because of the expenditure of money called for in assuming the Texas debt of $7,500,000, partly on account of the prevailing idea at the North that the new acquisition of territory was "to uphold the interests of slavery, extend its influence, and secure its permanent duration."

It was probably a great relief to President Tyler, whose administration had been so generally unacceptable to the country, when he could retire from office and enjoy his pleasant home at Sherwood Forest, Charles City County, Virginia, where he passed the years of his age in comfort, until the beginning of the Civil War in 1861. Then his old ideas of state rights and his advocacy of Mr. Calhoun's doctrines led him to join the Confederates. He was afterwards chosen a member of the Confederate Congress, but his death occurred at Richmond, January 18, 1862, and he never served in that body.

President Tyler was twice married, first to Miss Letitia Christian, who died in 1842, and was an invalid through much of her life. During his presidency, Mr. Tyler married Miss Gardiner of New York, whose father was killed by an explosion which occurred on the steamer Princeton, when Commodore Stockton was giving an entertainment to the government officials, the President being on board at the time, and two members of his Cabinet losing their lives by the disaster. The second Mrs. Tyler was a woman of distinguished appearance, who assumed more of the outward dignities of her position than any of her predecessors in the White House.

History is truth itself, but the records of nations are not history till time has separated the wheat from the chaff, until the years have weighed men's actions in an even balance, adjusting rightly those influences and currents of thought not taken into account by a hasty judgment or the sentiment of the hour. While his best friend could hardly justify President Tyler for his action in some of the important issues of the day, his greatest enemy would acknowledge the many praiseworthy characteristics of his public and private life. He was a man of the world in the best sense of the phrase; educated, not only in books, but in the school of experience. He was a firm friend to the small circle of intimates whom he loved, while he displayed eloquence and brilliancy, both in his familiar conversation and in his public speeches. His life was beset with many trials; he forfeited in later years the public confidence which he had held to so great a degree during his earlier political career, and he was tried in ways as unusual as they were severe. He would have been censured, whatever his course, even though it followed the best promptings of his nature, for his position, surrounded by difficulties, allowed of no popular way to overcome the murmurs and dissatisfaction incident to his administration. The world, very apt to give publicity to the failings of great men, will slowly learn to remember President Tyler for the virtues he displayed, those excellent traits of character which ought to do something towards blotting out the record of the many errors he so prominently exhibited during the later years of his public service.

JAMES K. POLK.

ELEVENTH PRESIDENT OF THE UNITED STATES.

JAMES KNOX POLK.

PRESIDENT, MARCH 4, 1845 — MARCH 4, 1849.

FAMILY NAME — PURSUIT OF KNOWLEDGE — GOOD HABITS — LEGAL STUDIES —
IN CONGRESS SEVEN SUCCESSIVE TERMS — SPEAKER OF THE HOUSE — GOV-
ERNOR OF TENNESSEE — PLEASANT HOME LIFE — MRS. POLK — ELECTED
PRESIDENT OVER HENRY CLAY — NOTABLE ACTS IN HIS ADMINISTRATION —
RETIREMENT FROM OFFICE — SICKNESS AND SUDDEN DEATH.

LANGUAGE, in maintaining a continuity of existence,
has merged within itself varied elements; the English
tongue has assimilated words and phrases from all cor-
ners of the earth. Many familiar names, common in America,
are corruptions, referring back to the time of the Norman con-
quest, or to the lands of the Celtic kings. Whenever the sons
of this new world can trace their ancestry through many generations, they may be sure that their name, perhaps in some
different form, has crossed the ocean from its former European
home, probably France or Great Britain. The ancestors of
James Polk were of Scoto-Irish origin; they bore the name of
Pollok, easily contracted into Polk by the family that left Ireland and settled in America some time during the eighteenth
century. The father of the future President was a farmer,
living in Mecklenburg County, North Carolina, when James
Knox Polk was born, November 2, 1795.

There were ten children to be reared in this home, removed
soon after the birth of the eldest son, James, to the region of
the Duck river in Tennessee. Samuel Polk, though a man of

small resources, possessed the spirit of enterprise, combined with energy, in all his pursuits. He actively engaged in the work of farming, occupying himself also with the duties of a surveyor, thus being able to comfortably provide for his large family, and, in later years, to amass a considerable fortune. The son James gained experiences connected with both these occupations, learned to endure the hardships of journeys through the wilderness of that region, as well as to conform to the more prosaic discipline connected with a boy's life on a farm. He early developed a fondness for nature, was also interested in his studies, while from both parents he received lessons of industry, thrift and promptness, necessary requisites for success in life.

The lad was a bright scholar, but not being physically strong, it was thought best that he should be fitted for some trade or business; accordingly he became a clerk, although having no liking for such occupation. He was so unhappy during a few weeks' trial of this kind of work, that his father decided to send him to Murfreesborough Academy, where he remained about two years, until prepared for the Sophomore class in college. He entered the University of North Carolina, on Chapel Hill, receiving high honors when he graduated therefrom in the year 1818.

When Mr. Polk left college his health was impaired, as a result of the close attention he had given to his studies, rest and change being needed that he might gain physical strength. After a brief period of leisure, he resumed his studies, this time those of law, under Mr. Felix Grundy of Nashville. He was admitted to the bar in 1820, and shortly afterwards began the practice of his profession in Columbia. At once success attended his efforts. His abilities, his logical powers of reasoning, his methodical habits, helped him greatly in becoming an eminent lawyer; not more so, perhaps, than that gracious charm of manner, that winning personality, which made him popular among his associates in society and business circles.

Mr. Polk's entrance into politics dates from the year 1823, when he was chosen to represent his county in the state legislature. He identified himself with the Republican party, and as a personal as well as a political friend of General Jackson, helped in the election of that distinguished man to the United States Senate. In August, 1825, Mr. Polk was chosen to represent his district in Congress, to which position he was re-elected every succeeding two years until 1839. He advocated the ideas of Jefferson and Jackson, being ranked as a democratic Republican of the strictest sect, holding persistently to his opinions throughout all party mutations. He opposed the administration of President John Quincy Adams, while he ardently supported in Congress the policy of President Jackson during his terms of service. Mr. Polk's reputation and influence were undoubtedly great, by reason of his extraordinary energy, his indomitable will, his powers of close application to whatever engaged his earnest attention.

His ten years' service in Congress fitted him for the elevated position of speaker, to which he was twice chosen by his associates, in the years 1835–7. In this important station there was opportunity to display all the skill of politician and statesman. Popular with his own party, Mr. Polk's abilities were recognized by many of his opponents; and his decisions as speaker upon questions of parliamentary law, many of them complex and difficult, were uniformly sustained.

In the year 1839, after fourteen years' service in Congress, during which time Mr. Polk was never absent from the sittings of the House, except on a single occasion, he declined to be a candidate for re-election. That same year he was elected governor of Tennessee; he served one term, but was defeated for re-election, and, on becoming a candidate, in 1843, again failed to secure the executive chair. He now enjoyed for a little time the quiet home life in the family circle where he displayed so many of the charming characteristics of his nature. He had married in his early manhood Miss Sarah Childers, of Tennessee, a woman of dignified personal appearance, who possessed much executive ability; was a notable housekeeper as well as an intelligent companion and admirable hostess. There were no children born to this couple, and when they occupied the White House it offered few attractions for youthful visitors, though it afforded cheerful surroundings for many older guests. Mr. Polk drew towards him numerous warm friends, for he possessed ready sympathies, had always a kind word of greeting, was courteous to everyone, betraying an honest interest in the well-being of his neighbors.

These uneventful years of Mr. Polk's life were followed by his nomination as a candidate for the presidency, Henry Clay being the opposing candidate. Mr. Polk was elected by a majority of sixty-five electoral votes. One of the main issues of the campaign was the annexation of Texas, a measure strongly advocated by Mr. Polk, and consummated by President Tyler just before the close of his presidential career. The new administration found itself confronted with many and serious difficulties growing out of this measure, and war with Mexico soon ensued. Mr. Polk felt the embarrassment of the situation, and much regretted the disruption of friendly relations with that country which occurred shortly after his inauguration. As a strong advocate of the annexation of Texas, he did not hesitate to join issue with Mexico in the alternative presented. He was in thorough accord with that section of the Democratic party which had done so much to bring about the result accomplished in the closing days of the administration of his immediate predecessor, and he was resolute to keep and defend the acquisition thus gained at all hazards. President Polk was sustained in his war policy against Mexico by a large majority in Congress, the whole force of the United States being placed at his disposal to enable him to prosecute the war to a speedy and successful termination.

In the Northern States the Mexican war was regarded with much disfavor, and the President lost popularity from this cause. In the Southwestern States, however, a different feeling prevailed; volunteers came readily to the aid of General Taylor, who led an army of some ten thousand soldiers across the border, fought several battles and gained signal victories. At a later date, General Scott, at the head of a victorious army, entered the capital and took possession of the city of Mexico. This was on Sept. 14, 1847. Negotiations for peace resulted in the "Treaty of Guadalupe Hidalgo," by which Mexico ceded New Mexico and California to the United States and agreed that the Rio Grande river should be the boundary line between herself and Texas, thus giving up a vast territory to this country. The United States government, however, by the terms of the treaty, agreed to pay to Mexico $15,000,000, besides paying all the claims of citizens of this country against Mexico. That President Polk was greatly elated over the results of the Mexican war cannot be doubted. We may well believe that he justified to himself the course pursued by this country in its aggressive dealings with Mexico, and wresting from her as the "spoils of war" such immense grants of territory; but had he been a less ardent upholder of slavery he would probably have been somewhat less enthusiastic both as regards the annexation of Texas and the prosecution of a war which was disapproved by so many of his countrymen.

Another act of his administration was of quite a different character. This was the settlement of the Oregon boundary dispute between Great Britain and the United States. President Polk believed the American title to be good to the whole territory, but favored a compromise, which was finally brought about, the boundary line being fixed at the forty-ninth degree of north latitude. In this adjustment of a long standing difference between the two nations the wise and conciliatory thought of the President was conspicuous. While he did not actually direct the negotiations resulting in the treaty made at Washington in June, 1846, and ratified by the Senate the same month, he yet made the influence of his own good judgment, not less than his official position, felt in the determination thus reached.

There were other acts belonging to the administration of President Polk that were of a most important and creditable character, and during the four years in which he held the highest office in the gift of the American people, our country gained wonderfully in many of the elements which mark material progress and prosperity. Three new states, Texas, Iowa and Wisconsin, were added to the Union; there were immense territorial acquisitions, together with a gratifying increase in wealth and population; and the influence of the President was recognized as a factor in many movements that tended to advance the Nation's glory and strength. He was an ardent upholder of slavery, however, and his views and acts had much to do with the deepening of feeling on that question — a feeling which in the North became so prominent in the last year of Mr. Polk's administration as to lead to the formation of the "Free Soil" party, out of which grew the Republican organization which finally obtained control of the government.

At the inauguration of President Taylor, Mr. Polk was a prominent figure. After joining heartily in the celebration incident to this occasion, the ex-President left Washington, intending to reach his home in Nashville, Tennessee, by a somewhat circuitous route. During his journey through several of the States he received ovations from his countrymen, as they honored, with appropriate demonstrations, the man of sterling worth who had given the best proof of his love for American institutions by rendering such efficient aid in their behalf during the long years of his public service.

His many friends at Nashville cordially welcomed Mr. Polk and his devoted wife, and the future seemed to hold in store for them many temporal blessings. The former President was comparatively a young man, but fifty-four years of age; with erect frame and great intellectual powers, he seemed destined to exert a helpful influence for a long period of time, although retired from the activity and anxieties attendant upon the holding of public office. His death, however, occurred shortly after his return to Nashville, June 15, 1849, when he sank peacefully to sleep at the close of several days of intense suffering. All through the Nation there was mourning for the death of so true a man; the honors paid to the distinguished dead were no empty tributes or meaningless forms, but expressed a sense of personal bereavement as well as grief for the Nation's loss.

The distinguishing characteristics of President Polk, shown in his student life, were as prominent during his later manhood as in the college days, when it was said of him that he was always prompt at every recitation, and gave the best attention possible to whatever was the occupation of the hour. These qualities of punctuality, promptness, and the power he possessed to concentrate his attention distinguished his career as a statesman, and made possible the best results of his untiring, well-directed energy. He was conscientious in fulfilling the tasks which lay nearest him, however unimportant they might seem to the casual observer, always showing that faithfulness to duty which was a part of his nature, revealed in his private life as well as during his term of service as President of the American Nation.

ZACHARY TAYLOR.

TWELFTH PRESIDENT OF THE UNITED STATES.

ZACHARY TAYLOR.

LIFE UNDER PRIMITIVE CONDITIONS — A SOLDIER FROM THE BEGINNING — LIEU-
TENANT IN THE AMERICAN ARMY — CONFLICT WITH THE INDIANS — THE
SEMINOLES IN FLORIDA — OFFICIAL RECOGNITION OF PATRIOTIC SERVICES —
HERO OF BUENA VISTA — UNEXPECTED NOMINATION — ELECTED PRESIDENT —
ONE YEAR'S RECORD — HIS DEATH — HONORABLE PLACE IN AMERICAN
HISTORY.

IN looking backward to the men foremost in establishing
this Republic, they compare favorably with those prominent in the American history of to-day. It is only when
we regard the outward conditions of this new world, then and
now, that we come to realize the great progress of the Nation
in all that makes for the best civilization. Men were heroes
and leaders in those early days; but the material resources,
now available for the service of American interests, were not
theirs to command, while the story of early struggles in the
wilderness indicates the great strides which comparatively few
years have witnessed in the material prosperity of our country. With a foundation into which has gone the sacrifice and
work of men honored in every time, the future results could
not fail to be those of successful achievement; but the rapid
growth in all the advantages of civilization has far exceeded
the limits prophesied of by the fathers. Up to the life time of
the twelfth President of this Republic the West and South
were lacking in many extrinsic aids to prosperity. Although

Zachary Taylor was born November 24, 1784, in Orange County, Virginia, his parents, the year following, removed to Louisville, Kentucky, and the lad was brought up in this little settlement, the humble beginning of the prosperous city which now bears the name.

This rough life, combined with the inherited tendencies from his father, a trusty soldier of the Revolution, brought out the military qualities and likings which were so soon apparent in the boyish nature. He was a soldier from the very beginning, not as all boys are who play with toy-drums and wear a miniature sword, but as one who fully realized what duty to his country meant, the hardships it involved. In the training as a farmer's boy, as well as during the little school education which he received, he was decisive and quick in his actions, somewhat blunt, yet frank in speech, honest in thought and deed, impetuous, ready to encounter personal risk, yet obedient, as he felt every true soldier ought to be.

Colonel Taylor was as much delighted as his son Zachary, when, in 1808, the young man, then twenty-four years of age, received a commission as Lieutenant in the United States army. There was no question in his mind as to whether or not he should accept the position; he felt that he was fitted for a soldier, and applying himself diligently to the duties required, he soon came to be regarded as a capable, trustworthy officer. It was about this time that he married Miss Margaret Smith, whose home was in Maryland.

The Indian attack led by the famous chief Tecumseh against Fort Harrison was an opportunity for Captain Taylor, who, in defense of the fort, gained distinction for his courage and skill. He was publicly complimented by General Hopkins for his conduct of this affair and was promoted to the rank of Major. His energy and coolness characterized his leadership in the various movements against the British and Indians, which were terminated by the restoration of peace with Great Britain, in 1815. At that time Major Taylor resigned his commission, his intention being to engage in agricultural pursuits for a time at his home in Louisville. After a year spent in this way he was re-instated in the army, resuming his duties with renewed ardor, rendering such efficient service that he was promoted to the rank of Colonel in 1832. He was extremely popular among the soldiers because he cheerfully bore his part with them in any danger or hardship, and had a stock of sound common sense which they could respect. His early opportunities had been few, but he had profited by his experiences; was skilled in Indian warfare; his habits of discipline and study still aided him, and he became an intrepid, wise commander.

The conduct of the Seminole war aroused much criticism in the United States because of an alleged undue harshness in dealing with that ferocious tribe of Indians. Its result, in the dispersion of the Seminoles to the west banks of the Mississippi caused general satisfaction, however, and was a signal victory for Colonel Taylor, who, by reason of his military skill and services in this connection, was elevated to the rank of Brigadier-General and appointed to the chief command of the army of the Southwest. During this time, while faithfully, yet in a very quiet manner, discharging his military duties, he bought a plantation near Baton Rouge, La., where he established his family in a comfortable, well cared for home.

It was not possible, however, for a military man like General Taylor to remain in obscurity while his country was agitated by the difficulties brought into prominence during the presidential campaign of 1844. Mr. Polk, a friend of slavery, and a pronounced champion of the annexation of Texas, was the successful candidate for election as President, and in this state of affairs it became apparent that war with Mexico was inevitable.   General Taylor was directed to hold his troops in readiness for service along the frontier.   He did this, but refused to enter upon aggressive measures to bring about a collision with Mexico, or to undertake any forward movements upon his own responsibility.   As a good soldier he waited for instructions and obeyed orders.   In March, 1846, in accordance with a command from President Polk, General Taylor advanced his army to the banks of the Rio Grande, claimed as the boundary line between Texas and Mexico.   The Mexican government had already ordered its troops to the same locality, so that it was evident a conflict must soon take place.

During the months of April and May, 1846, the American army met the enemy in several severe engagements, being victors in every case.   In his official reports concerning these battles General Taylor said: " Our victory has been decisive. A small force has overcome immense odds of the best troops that Mexico can furnish — veteran regiments perfectly equipped and appointed.   Eight pieces of artillery, several colors and standards, a great number of prisoners. including fourteen officers, and a large amount of baggage and personal property have fallen into our hands.   The causes of victory are doubtless to be found in the superior quality of our officers and men."

The conduct of the commanding officer in all these engagements was worthy of the praise it called forth from military men and those in authority.   Congress conferred the rank of Major-General upon the successful commander, and complimented his bravery by appropriate resolutions.   So much of confidence was felt in his abilities as a military leader that his troops were reinforced by volunteers, money and supplies were voted him, and he was thus prepared for the encounters which quickly followed.

The battle of Monterey was won by the Americans after

days of hard fighting, against great odds, both of position and
numbers, General Ampudia leading the defeated forces. General Taylor's course in treating with the Mexicans was criticised on the ground that he had allowed them too favorable
terms. This occasion of dissatisfaction with him, felt at Washington, together with the influence of political intrigues, perhaps, caused the order, given to a considerable part of General
Taylor's troops, that they should join the force of General
Scott, then about to attack Vera Cruz, preparatory to his con-
templated advance on the City of Mexico. General Taylor
showed his patriotism, his true soldierly instincts, by obeying
this order to send the best part of his troops to the support of
General Scott, changing his plans so as to stand, for the time,
only on the defensive.

General Santa Anna saw what seemed to be his opportunity to crush the reduced forces under General Taylor, and
moved rapidly upon them with his large, well-disciplined army,
giving battle at the pass of Buena Vista, February 22, 1847.
Although this encounter did not end the war, it being left with
General Scott to conduct skillful military operations until the
capital of Mexico was taken and the spirit of its people broken,
it was in fact the turning point of the long struggle, and properly ranks as one of the most notable battles in American history. During the two days' fighting at Buena Vista, General
Taylor displayed again his qualities of military leadership,
showing judgment in selecting the position for his men and in
directing their movements, while he inspired his troops to
bravery by his own courage and his coolness in confronting
the dangers to which he was constantly exposed.

The country, thoroughly awakened to the heroic virtues
of General Taylor, now rang with his praises; "Old Rough
and Ready" was transformed into the " hero of Buena Vista."
His growing fame and popularity caused him to be spoken of

as a candidate for the presidency. General Taylor distrusted
his fitness for that position. He had taken no part in political
affairs, had seldom voted, and had never held public office.
He was, however, nominated by the Whig Convention held in
Philadelphia, June 1, 1848, and elected President in the November following, over General Lewis Cass, the Democratic
candidate, and ex-President Van Buren, candidate of the Free
Soil party.

President Taylor was inaugurated at Washington, March
4, 1849, after having resigned his army commission with a
record for forty years' consecutive military service. He was
greatly tried and perplexed during his administration of political affairs. His training had not been that of a statesman or
political leader, but his natural shrewdness, his practical judgment, his insight into what was best for his country, enabled
him to do excellent service as the executive head of the government. The exciting questions of slavery were still agitated
through the land, the purchase of Cuba and the admission of
California caused much feeling and discussion. The President
helped still the waves of dissension, won the hearts of those
associated with him in administering the government, while his
countrymen generally appreciated his efforts to faithfully discharge the duties of his position, never shirking the responsibilities which at times weighed heavily upon him.

It was after a year of conflict, more trying to the great
soldier than all his encounters on the battle field, that President Taylor ended his mortal career, dying, after a brief illness, July 9, 1850, one year, four months, and five days after
his inauguration. Everywhere in the land there was mourning for the kindly man, the gallant soldier, who had so warm
a place in the affections of the American people.

The story of the Mexican war, possessed of much romantic historical interest, is inseparably connected with the fame

of General Taylor, making evident his prowess in the conduct of battles, and his reputation as a popular officer to whom his troops were personally attached. More frequently is he remembered as the hero of Buena Vista than as America's Chief Magistrate, though in the latter position he was far from being a nonentity or unfitted for his responsible duties. A true man is of value to his country whatever his capacities, if an honest heart beats in defense of his nation's liberty, of truth and the right. President Taylor was this and more. He was plain, simple in his tastes, possessed of little scholastic learning, yet his intellectual powers were not to be denied, his sound, practical wisdom not to be gainsaid. His life was not spent in the political arena, yet he had learned enough of statesmanship to skillfully grapple with the issues of the day, to shrewdly estimate men and affairs, so that he was not often misled or easily influenced. His pleasant, cordial manners did not proceed from a weak desire to court favor, but expressed his sympathetic feelings, which, however, did not lead him into errors of judgment or to vacillating opinions. As a quick, bold, decisive commander of armies, so he was an energetic, firm President, his true patriotism urging him to every service which his country might command. Carried into office by the enthusiasm which his great generalship had aroused, he did not allow himself to be regarded simply as the popular hero of the hour; he at once directed his energies to establishing his reputation as President upon something more enduring than the reflected glory of his military career; he was sincere, faithful to every trust committed to his keeping, a man of the people, a representative American, worthy to be enrolled among the noble few whose names are interwoven with the fibre of our national existence.

MILLARD FILLMORE.

THIRTEENTH PRESIDENT OF THE UNITED STATES.

MILLARD FILLMORE.

PRESIDENT, JULY 9, 1850 — MARCH 4, 1853.

LIMITED EDUCATION — APPRENTICED TO LEARN A TRADE — HELPED TO STUDY
LAW — EXTENSIVE LEGAL PRACTICE — IN LEGISLATURE AND CONGRESS —
COMPTROLLER OF NEW YORK — VICE-PRESIDENT — SUCCEEDED TO THE
PRESIDENCY — ADMINISTRATIVE POLICY AND RESULTS — LATER PERIOD OF
POLITICAL ACTIVITY — CANDIDATE OF THE "AMERICAN" PARTY FOR PRES-
IDENT — DEATH AT BUFFALO.

THE public school system of America, now so firmly established, has been of gradual growth, beginning in the
log cabins of the New World settlers, where teachers and
pupils together struggled with the "three R's," among primitive surroundings and with few facilities for the pursuit of
learning. The architectural pretensions of the modern school
buildings mark progress in the estimate placed upon the value
of a free education; but it must be remembered that in those
days there were pioneers of this movement, or the log cabin
school-houses would never have been builded by men forced
to work early and late to keep their families from absolute
want. Honor is due to those who believed in the benefits of a
public school education when the thought was not popular as
now; to those among the early settlers of our country who
fostered the germ which has ripened into the present broad
system, capable of such glorious results. One who thus appreciated the advantages of education was the father of Millard
Fillmore, thirteenth President of the United States. This
liberal-minded man, of Massachusetts origin, removed his fam-

8

ily to what is now Summer Hill, in Cayuga County, New York, in the year 1795, and the son, Millard, was born there, January 7, 1800.

This region was then but sparsely settled, the schools offered few advantages, books were expensive luxuries not to be indulged in by the farmers of that region, the most prosperous of whom were in somewhat humble circumstances. Both the parents of Millard Fillmore, however, encouraged his liking for intellectual pursuits and his desire for knowledge, though they could do little towards placing him in a position where his intelligent mind could be developed to its full extent. When a lad of fourteen years he was sent to a mill in Livingston County, to learn a clothier's trade. He was a diligent worker, but in his leisure hours he devoted himself to reading all the books available, specially those of travel, history, and biography. He thus rapidly trained his mental powers, while he acquired much information useful to him in his after life.

The lad of studious habits, quick intelligence and prepossessing appearance attracted the attention of Judge Wood, a man of kindly nature, who became friend and benefactor to the young clothier, taking him into his law office and giving him pecuniary aid for the pursuit of legal studies. Appreciating the advantages thus offered, Mr. Fillmore worked steadily in the way of preparation for several years under the guidance of Judge Wood, and afterwards in a law office of Buffalo, paying his necessary expenses in that city by teaching school. He was admitted to practice as a lawyer in 1823, and at that time established his residence in Aurora, Erie County, where his father had removed a few years before. In 1826 Mr. Fillmore married Miss Abigail Powers, the youngest child of Rev. Lemuel Powers of that village.

After a few years spent in a course of extended reading and the regular routine of a lawyer's life in a secluded village,

Mr. Fillmore returned to Buffalo and entered into partnership with two distinguished members of the bar in that city. Although his early education had been restricted, he partially made up for the defect by his diligence in the preparation of later years, so that, as opportunities were offered, he rapidly acquired a reputation for talents of a high order, for industry as well as ability in his profession.

During this period of his life Mr. Fillmore became actively interested in politics, having been chosen in 1829 a member of the State Legislature from Erie County. The Whig party, to which he belonged, was then in the minority in New York, nevertheless he exerted considerable influence, and was the principal mover in helping to secure the passage of the law abolishing imprisonment for debt, his speeches on the subject winning admiration for their clear, logical presentation of the matter. He continued to ably serve his constituents in the House of Assembly until 1832, when, in the autumn of that year, he was elected to Congress. In this capacity his abilities were more widely recognized, as there were greater opportunities for the display of intellectual gifts and political acquirements. But in this body, as in the State Legislature, Mr. Fillmore, being in the minority, was unable to render any large service, or make himself specially conspicuous, though he performed all his Congressional duties with characteristic faithfulness.

With the expiration of his term of office he resumed the practice of law in Buffalo, continuing it for two years. In 1836 he again consented to be a candidate, and was re-elected to Congress, being kept in that office by successive elections until 1842, when he declined further service. During these later years of his Congressional career, he held a foremost position as one of the leaders of his party, was popular throughout the State, and acquired a national reputation. He was painstaking and industrious in performing the duties incident to his position; he was skilled in debate, the solid basis of legal knowledge which he possessed enabling him to discuss public interests without special preparation. He was called to responsible labors as chairman of the Committee on Ways and Means, an office which required all the intellectual resources, the quick perceptions, the constant attention which he devoted to its service. During his several terms in office he was identified with many notable measures. He held pronounced views in the matter of protection, and was influential in securing many of the provisions incorporated into the tariff of 1842. Naturally conservative in feeling, he yet favored the restriction of slavery in the District of Columbia, the abolition of the slave trade between the States, and stood with John Quincy Adams in support of the rights of all persons, including women and slaves, to petition Congress. He left his place in the House of Representatives with an honorable record for his work in behalf of his country's interests, while his retirement from office was deplored by his party and constituents.

For a brief period only was Mr. Fillmore relieved from an active participation in political affairs, for in 1844 he was nominated by the Whig party as candidate for Governor of New York. He was defeated, however, after an exciting canvass, by the opposing candidate, Mr. Silas Wright; but he drew to his support the full strength of his party. In 1847 he was elected State Comptroller. He resigned his lucrative professional practice in Buffalo to assume this position, removing to Albany shortly after his election, that he might better discharge the labors which devolved upon the incumbent of that important public trust.

Mr. Fillmore at this period was popular with his party, both in New York and beyond its limits. He had made an excellent record, and shown many statesmanlike qualities. His gen-

eral reputation was that of a wise and skillful political leader,
who well deserved to be called to a higher place than any he
had yet filled. When the Whig Convention met at Harris-
burg, Pennsylvania, in June, 1848, to nominate candidates for
President and Vice-President, it selected for the first office
General Zachary Taylor, famous as a soldier, but untrained in
civil matters, and greatly deficient in knowledge of political
affairs. In view of this selection it was thought best to associate with the popular soldier a man versed in government
matters and more of a statesman, and therefore Millard Fillmore, holding the esteem of his party, was its choice as candidate for Vice-President. The election of 1848 resulted in the
success of the Whig ticket, General Taylor and Mr. Fillmore
being inaugurated in their respective positions March 4, 1849.

As the presiding officer of the Senate, Vice-President Fillmore showed marked ability, was dignified, firm, and always
maintained order and decorum in debate. The exciting question of slavery aroused great interest on both sides. Party
feeling was intense, the whole country was in a fevered condition; there were strong men in the Senate, and to preside over
its deliberations called for more than ordinary mental equipment, but Mr. Fillmore was able to meet all the requirements
which the position demanded. After this preparation there
was soon to ensue a more responsible and trying charge.
President Taylor died July 9, 1850, and Mr. Fillmore was his
constitutional successor in office.

Thus unexpectedly called to assume the arduous duties of
this exalted station, it yet seemed that Mr. Fillmore had special
fitness for the discharge of the duties thus devolved upon him.
He encountered many difficulties during the nearly three years
of his career as Chief Magistrate, one obstacle being that the
party in opposition was in the majority in both Houses of
Congress for the greater part of this time. President Fillmore

did not win the entire approbation of his party associates, much less of the people of the country. He disappointed the expectations of the North by approving the Fugitive Slave Law, and issuing a proclamation calling upon government officials to enforce its provisions. The various compromise measures regarding slavery adopted during his administration were by no means successful in conciliating the South, while they intensified the anti-slavery opinions of the North and resulted in the disruption of the Whig party.

Among the pleasant features which were notably associated with the nearly three years in which President Fillmore was at the head of the government, were the reception of the Hungarian patriot, Kossuth, the sending of an embassy, under Commodore Perry, to Japan, the passage of an act securing cheaper rates of postage for the American people. In recalling the history of this administration, not altogether a successful one, the discretion, faithfulness and ability of the President are now admitted, however much of adverse criticism some of his acts may seem to deserve. In the clearer judgment of to-day more allowance is made for the mistakes he committed, while it is seen that these mistakes are offset by the earnest efforts he made to promote good feeling between the different sections of the country and to advance its interests. It is now generally conceded that he was "always honest, capable, and faithful to the constitution."

Just before the expiration of his term of office Mrs. Fillmore died. The President, accompanied by his son and daughter, left Washington soon after the inauguration of his successor, and again entered upon the life of a private citizen in Buffalo. In 1858 he married Mrs. Carolina M'Intosh, of Albany, and not afterwards taking an active part in public affairs, he was able to enjoy his home and follow the quiet pursuits in which he took so much delight.

His views upon the questions of national interest were often sought, and sometimes freely given. On several occasions after his retirement from the Presidency he was called upon for public addresses, in which he avowed his opinions in a way to command attention. In one of these addresses he expressed a wish that both Canada and Mexico might be annexed to the United States. At one time he was prominent in the Native American party, and was named as its candidate for President. When the storm of Civil War broke upon the land Mr. Fillmore kept silence. Neither then, nor afterward during the four years' struggle, did he speak the approving word which would have been most encouraging to patriotic hearts at a time when the American Union was in direst peril.

The ex-President died March 8, 1874, in Buffalo, New York, that city having been his residence for much the greater part of his life. He was held in high esteem by those who stood nearest to him — his neighbors, associates and personal friends. Whatever differing regard there may be as to some acts of his public career, this approving estimate is greatly to his credit. There can be no question as to the uprightness which marked his private life, nor the conscientious devotion with which he applied himself to the discharge of all official trusts. His plain, simple manners were never altered by the honors which he received, and his dignified, courteous bearing was the same throughout his long life, in the various conditions and circumstances by which he was influenced. To a man of this stamp there is due a meed of praise because of his intelligent labors, however much of criticism may attach to his plans of work, ideas of public policy, and some of his official acts.

FRANKLIN PIERCE.

FOURTEENTH PRESIDENT OF THE UNITED STATES.

FRANKLIN PIERCE.

PRESIDENT, MARCH 4, 1853 — MARCH 4, 1857.

ANCESTRAL INHERITANCE — STUDENT AT BOWDOIN COLLEGE — STUDIES LAW
UNDER JUDGE WOODBURY — ENTERS THE FIELD OF POLITICS — SUCCESSFUL
PROFESSIONAL CAREER — SERVICES IN THE MEXICAN WAR — NOMINATION
FOR THE PRESIDENCY — ADMINISTRATION OF THE PRESIDENTIAL OFFICE —
RETIREMENT AND HOME — CAUSES OF PERSONAL POPULARITY AND PROFES-
SIONAL SUCCESS.

IN this land of ours, where the distinctions between the rich
and poor are not so marked as in the older nations, the
home life of all its families has much in common. From
these homes arises a bond of union, linking together lives which
share the domestic atmosphere surrounding alike the fireside
groups in the mansion of the millionaire, and those in the poor
man's humble cottage. The early American settlers did more
than eke out a scanty existence on the shores of the New
World; they founded homes whose influence has extended
until the present day, a means of strength and blessing to the
Nation. That this common sympathy exists is proved by the
interest shown in the private life of distinguished citizens, as
well as by the fact that biography deals more and more largely
with the surroundings, conditions, the birthplace and home life
of its subject, instead of closely confining itself to public
events or the incidents contributing to a national reputation.

Among the happy homes situated among the hills of New England four score years ago, was that of General Pierce, a soldier in the Revolution, afterwards an energetic citizen who had acquired some little property, had made for his family a comfortable dwelling-place, and was honored by several responsible public positions, among them that of Governor of his State, just tributes to his intelligence and worth. His wife helped in the establishment of that home, was true-hearted, prudent and refined, a faithful companion, a loving, wise, and devoted mother. Here, in Hillsborough, New Hampshire, November 23, 1804, was born Franklin Pierce, the fourteenth President of the United States.

This boy, one of a family of eight children, was a bright and promising lad, entering Bowdoin College, Brunswick, Maine, when sixteen years old. During the four years spent in college he was noted for his agreeable, courteous manners, which attracted to him many friends among the students and those connected with the institution. Two of the acquaintances made thus early in his career were the poet Longfellow and the gifted writer Hawthorne, who, associated with him in college days, continued to be his life-long friends.

After his graduation from Bowdoin, in 1824, he studied law under the direction of Judge Woodbury, of Portsmouth, afterwards with Judge Parker, of Amherst, his admission to the bar occurring in the year 1827. In addition to his professional interests, Mr. Pierce was early inclined to take active part in politics. An ardent Democrat, he warmly supported the general principles of his party, and earnestly advocated, by speech and with his pen, the election of General Jackson to the presidency. Mr. Pierce's official political labors dated from his entrance into the State Legislature, in 1829. He served in this capacity for several terms, being chosen speaker of that body in the year 1832, an office for which he was specially qualified by reason of his gifts, and which he filled to the general acceptance. Elected in 1833 to Congress, he gained little influence and did not attract much attention for his services in this direction. He was, however, popular throughout his State, as was shown by his election to the United States Senate in 1837. While there he gained no conspicuous rank, though he was able in debate, and conscientious in his performance of all official duties.

In the year following his election as Senator Mr. Pierce married Miss Jane Means Appleton, and enjoyed establishing, with her aid, a pleasant home at Concord, the capital of his native State. He resigned his position as Senator in the year 1842, engaging in the practice of his profession, achieving more than ordinary success. He declined at this time the offer of a position in the Cabinet of President Polk, also refusing the proffered nomination as candidate for Governor of New York. He now devoted thought and energies to his large law practice, evincing an excellent quality of mind, as well as the possession of many legal accomplishments, in caring for his clients' interests. He achieved wonderful success as a lawyer, his popularity doubtless depending not only upon the mental powers and intellectual training which he displayed, but also upon his gracious, urbane manners; his great personal magnetism influencing juries as it influenced all his associates. Never was a man more courteous in his treatment of friends and foes; he was always calm, moderate, and even-tempered, however trying the occasion or vexatious the circumstances.

At the beginning of the Mexican War, Mr. Pierce joined the army of volunteers, enlisting in a company raised in Concord. Soon commissioned Colonel of the Ninth Regiment, another promotion to the rank of Brigadier-General followed quickly in his military career, as his leadership gave evidence of skill, resolution and bravery. He took part in the battles of Contreras and Molino del Rey, accompanying General Scott to the City of Mexico, the capture of which virtually ended the war.

General Pierce returned to his home during December of 1847, after these services in defense of his country, entering again upon the professional duties which were waiting his attention. In 1850, he occupied a prominent position as presiding officer in the convention called to revise the constitution of New Hampshire. Two years later he was made the standard bearer of the Democratic party, and elected President by a large majority, only four States casting their electoral votes against him.

Sorrow quickly followed upon the election of President Pierce, his only son, a boy of twelve years, being killed in a railway accident, the mother witnessing the horrible disaster, yet powerless to aid her beloved boy. The blow of sudden bereavement fell upon Mr. Pierce with a terrible severity, while it almost crushed his sorrowing wife. From that time forward she carried a saddened, weary heart, and though she tried to cast off the gloom which encircled her life, she was yet greatly changed by this event, which touched the hearts of all who knew its details, and brought into expression a tender sympathy for the parents thus sorely afflicted.

Mr. Pierce entered upon the office of President March 4, 1853, under conditions which seemed to indicate a pleasant and successful administration. He had been elected by an unusually large majority. The party which supported him was strong and confident, while the opposite was divided and dispirited. The material prosperity of the country excelled that of any former period. For a brief time the excitement regarding the disturbing questions of slavery was lessened. It was thought by many that the compromise measures would ensure a permanent settlement of these questions. An era of internal peace and mutual good feeling between the North and the South was confidently anticipated. There was not to be, however, a full realization of such expectations. President Pierce, by the terms of his inaugural address, left no doubt as to his purpose to support slavery in the United States, while he announced his resolve that the Fugitive Slave Act should be strictly enforced. Thus President Pierce sounded forth the key-note of his administration, the result being a renewal of agitation, an increase of hostile feeling between the North and the South, giving indications of a struggle that was close at hand. The repeal of the Missouri Compromise, the attempt to establish slavery in Kansas and to strengthen it elsewhere, augmented the feeling between the two sections. The President acted upon the policy that everything must be done to conciliate the South and thus avert consequences so much to be dreaded. Thus he went to the extreme in sanctioning the irregular measures by which slavery was nominally established in Kansas. The people of that territory resisted the imposition, however, and the slave-holding interest was finally defeated, although not without a great cost of suffering and hatred.

In nearly all the acts of his administration, as related to the subject of slavery, President Pierce went contrary to the general feeling of the North, pursuing a policy of conciliation to the South that was not altogether satisfactory to many of his own party. His course in dealing with these questions, together with the legislation of that period respecting slavery, stimulated the growth of the Republican party, which, at the expiration of his term of office, became clothed with the elements of an abiding political power. It is pleasant, however, to consider in this connection other acts of President Pierce's administration which stand very much to his credit. His conduct of foreign affairs, William L. Marcy being Secretary of State, merited and received general commendation. The firmness shown by the American government in the case of Martin Kosta was much praised, and the action taken in securing a treaty with Japan was regarded in the same favorable light. The purchase of the vast regions of Arizona and New Mexico has been justified in what has since been shown of the needs and progress of our country, while the price, $10,000,000, was but a small sum to pay for 45,000 square miles of territory.

President Pierce failed to receive the nomination of his party for re-election, Mr. Buchanan being selected as the Democratic candidate, and elected after an exciting canvass. The retiring President left Washington on the inauguration of his successor, and soon after traveled extensively through Europe. Returning from his protracted journeying, he settled at his home in Concord, New Hampshire, where he passed the remainder of his mortal life, taking no active part in political affairs. He died October 8, 1869.

One of President Pierce's distinguishing characteristics was the steadfastness which he showed in his friendships. He attached himself very deeply to those whom he thought merited his confidence, believing in them so strongly that he was willing to hear no criticism of their actions from others, though perhaps he admitted to himself that it was deserved. Reference has been made to his notable friendship with Longfellow and Hawthorne; he held also the kindest relations with many of his official associates, Senator Benton specially winning his esteem, though at one time political differences of opinion threatened estrangement. President Pierce's actions in behalf of the Senator, however, gave proof that his friendly feeling always remained the same, for as Mr. Benton said: "It is Pierce's head that is wrong — his heart is always right."

The cheerful, social qualities of this representative man were best shown in his personal life, where he delighted in the meeting of congenial acquaintances and exercised a most cordial hospitality. There was something attractive in his bearing which caused even strangers to feel the warmth of his personality and be induced to linger in his presence. As a lawyer his popularity was wonderful; men liked to hear his words upon any subject, and unconsciously were influenced by that charm which pervaded his being. These amiable graces which he exercised were more powerful to win for him success, than more striking qualities of greatness would have been; they appealed directly to the hearts of men, and did not shock them, as genius sometimes does, into a forced appreciation of its greatness. While not underrating President Pierce's intellectual abilities, it may be justly said that in his human sympathies, his warm heart, his courteous demeanor, was hidden the secret of his success in life; the sweetness of disposition which entered into his manly, upright nature, would have made him a noticeable character, even had he not been exalted to the high rank of a political leader, and called upon to assume the helm of national affairs.

JAMES BUCHANAN.

FIFTEENTH PRESIDENT OF THE UNITED STATES.

JAMES BUCHANAN.

PRESIDENT, MARCH 4, 1857—MARCH 4, 1861.

NATURE pleases us most when she furnishes a background for historical or biographical incidents; when there is associated with the grandeur of her mountains or the quiet loveliness of her valleys, some human interest, leading to that " proper study of mankind," as connected with the gracious influences of the outward world. When the boyhood of James Buchanan, fifteenth President of the United States, is recalled, there arises a thought of the lofty Alleghany Mountains, whose peaks overshadowed the secluded farm-house, situated in a little settlement of Franklin County, Pennsylvania, where he was born April 23, 1791. As soon as he was allowed to explore the wooded region near his home he spent much of his time out of doors, learning in his childhood days to appreciate the beauties which Nature so lavishly displays for her admirers. His mother, having an artistic nature, an inherent love for the beautiful, encouraged and educated her son's taste for the refinements of life, although in that simple frontier home it was not easy to acquire luxuries or receive

9

the benefits of books and cultured society. About the year
1800 these thoughtful parents removed their family to the
town of Mercersburg, that they might secure more of educa-
tional and social advantages for their son, an intelligent, interesting, somewhat precocious lad. Thus early separated from
his beloved mountains and the forests where the settler's axe
had but recently resounded, he never forgot, during the varied
experiences of his after life, the surroundings of his early
home, the intercourse with Nature which distinguished his boyhood days.

Having made rapid progress in his studies, James Buchanan
entered Dickenson College, at Carlisle, Pennsylvania, and
graduated with honor from that institution when he was
eighteen years old. At once he began the study of law, was
admitted to the bar in 1812, and established his legal practice
in the city of Lancaster, rapidly gaining reputation as an able
advocate, in spite of his youth and inexperience. Important
cases were entrusted to his care, and his treatment of them
more than justified expectation. "At the age of thirty years,"
says one of his biographers, "it was generally admitted that
he stood at the head of the bar, and there was no lawyer in
the State who had a more extensive or lucrative practice."

When, in 1820, he entered Congress, where he remained
for five successive terms, he was obliged to relinquish a large
proportion of his practice in order to perform the services
devolving upon his official position. As a member of the State
Legislature, in 1814, he had urged the vigorous prosecution
of the war of 1812, and while originally a Federalist, his opinions changed somewhat, so that he came to advocate the Jeffer-
sonian idea of a strict construction of the powers granted the
general government. Naturally he allied himself with the
Republican, afterwards the Democratic party, taking ground
against a protective tariff, and in opposition to the general

policy of President John Quincy Adams, while he warmly
espoused the measures advocated by General Jackson. At
the completion of his fifth term he retired from Congress, having
earned a reputation for a sound judgment, a wisely-directed
activity, made apparent in all labors for the State or Nation
which he had been called upon to perform.

Appointed Minister Plenipotentiary to St. Petersburg, in
the year 1832, Mr. Buchanan was able to negotiate, in his representative capacity, a commercial treaty, securing to the
United States important privileges in the Baltic and the Black
Sea. On his return to this country the Pennsylvania Legislature elected him to a seat in the United States Senate. Among
such representative men as Webster, Clay, Calhoun and
Wright, his influence was yet felt, and he gained a position
well to the front, among the foremost leaders of his party. In
matters where the interests of slavery were involved he was
generally inclined to favor the demands of the South, although
it is to be remembered to his credit that he supported President Jackson in his course against nullification. Mr. Buchanan
took the position that Congress had no power to legislate on
slavery, but evidently he was willing to perpetuate and extend
the system, and to bring Congressional influence to bear upon
such extension.

At the period of President Van Buren's administration,
Mr. Buchanan gave his earnest advocacy to the measures proposed by the National Executive, notably, that important action
respecting the establishment of an independent treasury. In
1845, he accepted the invitation of President Polk to enter his
Cabinet, where, as Secretary of State, his abilities found ample
and congenial scope. With the retirement of Mr. Polk from
the Presidency there came to Mr. Buchanan a welcome relief
from official duties and the activities of political interests.
After enjoying for several years the life of a private citizen,

he was summoned therefrom by President Pierce, who appointed him Minister to Great Britain. While abroad in the fulfillment of his mission, he joined Messrs. Mason and Soule, Ministers respectively to France and Spain, in a conference at Ostend, which resulted in the issue of a manifesto, proposing the acquisition of Cuba, by purchase or otherwise. This Ostend Manifesto, which caused great excitement in the United States and Europe, reflected but little honor upon Mr. Buchanan, the originator of the movement.

Upon returning to his native land, in 1856, Mr. Buchanan became the candidate of the Democratic party for the Presidency. He was elected over ex-President Fillmore, candidate of the American party, and John C. Fremont, supported by the newly formed Republican organization, to which were attached many members of the Whig and Free Soil parties.

In many respects President Buchanan was eminently fitted for the high position to which he was called by the American people. He had native and acquired ability, a large and varied experience, and was familiar with all departments of the public service. He was confronted, however, by unusual difficulties, so that he was tested to an extreme degree. His administration was unique and eventful from its beginning to its exciting close. A condition of affairs amounting almost to war existed for the greater part of the time, and new perils were constantly appearing. There was an inheritance of the Kansas-Nebraska imbroglio, with other questions of a troublesome character. Soon followed the Dred Scott Decision, which greatly intensified the anti-slavery feeling by declaring the right of slave-holders to take their slaves into any State and hold them there as such, despite any local law to the contrary. This decision, regarded as changing slavery from a local to a national institution, acted as a new stimulus to the agitation which President Buchanan vainly hoped to quiet.

The famous raid of John Brown, in 1859, produced the greatest excitement throughout the country. The leader was a brave, conscientious man, of noble impulses, but fanatical to the extreme regarding slavery. His ambition was to be a liberator, and his raid at Harper's Ferry was designed to force the issue and bring on a general uprising of the slaves. It was impossible that such a movement as that which he inaugurated should succeed. He and his associates were soon captured by a United States military force, and the brave leader paid the penalty of his mistaken ardor with his life. The movement, however, and all that went with it and followed, tended to widen the breach between the North and the South, and augment the difficulties of Mr. Buchanan, who was seeking to do a work of pacification, for which the time had passed.

There were other troubles with which the President had to deal, besides those directly relating to slavery. The Walker filibustering expeditions gave him much annoyance; but these movements terminated with the capture of Walker, who was tried and executed by the military authorities of Honduras. There were likewise old questions of a complicated nature pertaining to foreign affairs; and, in his dealing with these issues, President Buchanan was remarkably fortunate. He caused the English government to abandon its alleged right to search American ships — a claim, the attempted enforcement of which caused the war of 1812. This was a most satisfactory settlement of a question that had been one of frequent irritation between the two countries.

As the administration of President Buchanan approached its close, the aspect of affairs grew more threatening; the South being determined to withdraw from the Union and establish a separate government. When the Presidential election of 1860, which resulted in the choice of Mr. Lincoln, was decided, there was no longer hesitancy in going forward with the move-

ments of secession.   Forts were seized, public property appro-
priated, and various measures instituted and actively entered
upon which were intended to result in the disruption of the
Union.   The President was halting and irresolute at this critical juncture.   He was neither bold nor prompt enough in his
action to meet the emergency.   He hesitated, and counseled
inactivity when he should have moved forward to check the
attempted movement of disunion.

President Buchanan declared in his address to Congress, of
December, 1860, that no State had the right to secede from the
Union; but he doubted his own powers to coerce a sovereign
State, though he thought he could protect the Federal forts and
prevent their capture.   He tried to do this at the last, but was
unable to keep Forts Sumter and Moultrie in Charleston Harbor from passing into Confederate hands.   He did not believe
that the Constitution gave him the power which he would like
to use against secession.   He was not cast in heroic mould,
and could not deal with the impending crisis as a bolder man,
one not carrying so great a weight of years, and by nature
less conservative, would have done.   He did not wish to bring
on civil war, albeit the very course he took may have tended
to that result.   No doubt he misapprehended the situation and
showed a lack of firmness, but there is no proof that he was
at heart unpatriotic, or that consciously he wrought in aid of
secession.   After the organization of the Confederacy he still
hoped that it might prove a "rope of sand," and the way to an
honorable compromise would open.

The retiring President remained in Washington to witness
the inauguration of his successor in office, Abraham Lincoln,
shortly afterwards going to his home in Wheatland, Pennsylvania, where he passed the uneventful years until the time
of his death, June 1, 1868.   During this period he prepared
and published a defense of his administration, an interesting

work, throwing much light upon the question at issue and the motives by which his actions were guided. This defense confirmed the estimate now so generally placed upon his character, that he was not unpatriotic in feeling or purpose, and that he was opposed to the principles of secession. The judgment hastily given concerning President Buchanan during his lifetime, seems more harsh than is warranted by the facts presented in the clearer light of dispassionate, historical record to-day. His mistakes and errors were many, but his surroundings called for exceptional qualities rarely combined in the individual life, and few men, situated as he was, would have been equal to the demand.

Among the many offices of public trust that Mr. Buchanan filled, he served perhaps the most acceptably in his diplomatic relations with foreign countries. He was distinguished in his bearing, had much grace and tact in his intercourse with the representative men from different nations, and was more firm in negotiation when representing his country's interests abroad than in his policy to preserve the American Union.

Although criticised so widely, his moral character was never assailed, amid all the bitterness of denunciation which attacked his public career. He was never married, but he had an underlying vein of tenderness in his nature, possessed a kindly, genial disposition, was most interesting in conversation, a pleasant acquaintance, a true friend. Called to the Presidency at a most trying time in the Nation's history, he ought not to be judged apart from the environments of his position, which should serve as excuses for some of his errors, while throwing into greater prominence the virtues of his unsullied character, his acknowledged integrity, his abilities and activities.

ABRAHAM LINCOLN.

SIXTEENTH PRESIDENT OF THE UNITED STATES.

ABRAHAM LINCOLN.

ANCESTRY — BOYHOOD LIFE AND STRUGGLES — CLERK AND SURVEYOR — STUDIES
LAW — ADMISSION TO THE BAR — ELECTED TO THE LEGISLATURE — TO CON-
GRESS — FIRM STAND AGAINST SLAVERY — DEBATES WITH SENATOR DOUG-
LAS — ELECTION TO THE PRESIDENCY — ADMINISTRATION — EMANCIPATION
PROCLAMATION — SECOND ELECTION — ASSASSINATION — CHARACTER AND
SERVICES.

BETTER than written description is that statue standing
in Lincoln Park, Chicago, to indicate the true expression of a life, familiar in its details to the American
people, yet a character whose depths were never sounded in
any study of its many-sided development. The bronze figure
of Abraham Lincoln not only reproduces his physical attributes, but the artist has brought out, in a right conception of
what the statue should reveal, the greatness of the man, sug-
gesting, by the expression and the attitude, that personality
which a biography sometimes fails to present. In the sympathetic treatment of so difficult a subject, the sculptor has produced an instantaneous picture, a composite representation,
embodying the uncouth lad, the diligent surveyor, the useful
lawyer, the skilled leader of debate, the Nation's Chief Magistrate, and its martyred hero,— while above all shines the glory
of simple, honest virtues, the goodness as well as the greatness that was his. Thus the statue emphasizes the biographical teachings of an individuality, potential not only by reason
of its opportunities, but from its inherent moral balance; that

wonderful spirit, enveloped in so rough an exterior, which ex-
panded, in dignity and simplicity, among all the rude and
unfriendly influences to which the life of Lincoln was subjected.

Diligent search has revealed but little concerning the life
of Thomas Lincoln, the father of Abraham, the fragments of
biography, however, being sufficient to indicate the toil and
suffering by which his life was bounded. In the midst of the
dense forest on Nolin Creek, of what is now La Rue County,
Kentucky, Thomas Lincoln and his young wife built a home,
a rude log cabin, where their son Abraham was born February
12, 1809.

The boyhood of Lincoln offers an inviting field, but it must
not be enlarged upon within the limits of this sketch. It included an early childhood spent in the backwoods; an immi-
gration with his family to Indiana; the loss of a dearly-loved
mother; the advent of a step-mother who was truly a parent
to the neglected children; a limited education in books, but
the using of every opportunity for study, so that he learned to
read and write; another removal of the family to Illinois, and
the rough, laboring life of a new frontier settlement. Mrs.
Lincoln's testimony that " Abe " was a good boy, was in harmony with the general tribute paid to his generous, amiable
qualities, his defense of weaker, down-trodden humanity, of
cruelly-used animals, his straightforwardness, his determined
will, and his energy as displayed in those boyhood years passed
in poverty and hard work.

Having attained his majority and aided in the establishment of a new home for his parents, the young man went forth
to seek occupation and begin the shaping of a career which in
its progress was to be invested with a marvellous power and
attractiveness. He first engaged himself as a laborer to work
on a farm near his father's residence. There he was employed

a part of his time in building fences, so that in the political campaigns of late years he was frequently designated as the "railsplitter" of Illinois. Then he went to Springfield, the shire town of Sangamon County, and since made the capital of Illinois, where he wrought in the construction of a large flatboat, which he helped to guide down the Sangamon, Illinois, and Mississippi rivers to New Orleans. Returning from this trip, he worked in a country store at New Salem, Illinois, gaining the confidence of the people, who quickly discerned his abilities and manly work. In 1832, at the breaking out of the Black Hawk War, young Lincoln promptly volunteered, and was chosen to be captain of the companies raised in Sangamon County. While he did not participate in any battle, he yet bore the hardships of the three months' campaign in so brave and uncomplaining a way that he returned to New Salem with his popularity deservedly augmented. At this period, besides performing the duties devolving upon him, he was studying surveying, becoming so well fitted for this work that in 1838 he was appointed a deputy of the county surveyor.

Mr. Lincoln's political career may be said to date from the year 1834, when he was elected to the Illinois Legislature. He belonged to the Henry Clay school of politics, and was in sympathy with the general policy of the Whig party. His legislative course, which lasted through four successive terms, was marked by energy and ability, united with an earnest purpose to maintain the rights of the poor and oppressed, and do exact justice to all classes. About the time of his first election, Mr. Lincoln began to pursue a course of reading, with a view of entering the legal profession. He was admitted to the bar in 1836, and the next year removed to Springfield, where he was associated with his friend and adviser, Mr. John T. Stuart, in a practice that soon became extensive and lucrative. Mr. Lincoln achieved success in the practice of law, especially in his conduct of cases before juries. He was eloquent and persuasive in speech, logical and convincing, yet noted for his fairness in the treatment of an opponent. His integrity was never questioned. His entire faithfulness to a cause or principle which he had espoused was always conceded. He won his way slowly, but surely, to a prominent place, being ranked as an upright, hard-working, capable lawyer, in whose hands the most important interests might be safely reposed. Although giving the most of his time to his law practice, he still retained an active interest in local politics. In 1846 he was elected to Congress and served one term.

The abrogation of the Missouri Compromise in 1854 deeply affected Mr. Lincoln, and from that time forward he made frequent and strong expressions of his views on the subject of slavery. He became identified with the Republican party at its formation, taking, as of right, a place among its foremost leaders. In 1858, when the senatorial term of Mr. Douglas was near its close, Mr. Lincoln was put forward for the succession. In accordance with a general feeling, the two candidates arranged for a public discussion, which excited great attention throughout the country, and did much to enhance the reputation of Mr. Lincoln. He did not succeed in obtaining the senatorship, although a majority of the popular vote was in his favor, but he attained distinction by his method of treating the slavery question, going to the very heart of this disturbing issue, and dealing with the moral element. He was not an abolitionist; he was not inclined to disturb slavery in any rights that it might have under the Constitution in the States where it existed, but he boldly opposed its further encroachments. He had the clear vision to see what the issue would be. Thus he declared in one of his addresses in 1858: "A house divided against itself cannot stand. I believe this Government cannot endure permanently half slave and half free. I do not expect the Union to be dissolved — I do not expect the house to fall — but I do expect it will cease to be divided."

As the time drew near for the holding of the Republican Convention to nominate candidates respectively for the offices of President and Vice-President, the name of Mr. Lincoln was sometimes mentioned for one or the other place. The skill which he had shown in his debates with Senator Douglas was generally conceded, and yet he was not regarded with that measure of general favor accorded to Mr. Seward and others who had been largely instrumental in the formation of the Republican party. In the early part of 1860 Mr. Lincoln visited the East, speaking in New York and elsewhere with so much of intellectual and moral force as to command special attention. Thenceforth he became more widely known, and a much higher estimate was put upon his powers. It was hardly thought possible, however, that he could secure the nomination for the Presidency at the hands of the Convention which met in Chicago May 16, 1860; but on the third ballot he received more votes than were given for all his distinguished competitors, and under the pressure of an intense feeling of enthusiasm his nomination was made unanimous.

Then followed a bitter political contest, resulting in the election of Mr. Lincoln, who received 180 electoral votes, the remaining 123 being divided among the opposing candidates. During all the heated canvass, and the threatening days following his election, Mr. Lincoln bore himself with composure, making expression, however, not infrequently, of the resolute fibre of which his nature was formed. His letters, written at the time, show how far-seeing his vision was, and how quick and strong his impulses of patriotic devotion. Possessed of a deeply religious nature, he had a firm reliance upon Divine Providence, and believed that thus he was to be led and upheld in the arduous path of official duty. Preserved from dangers of one sort and another, Mr. Lincoln was duly inaugurated as the Chief Magistrate of the Nation. His inaugural address, while it declared "the Union perpetual and all acts of secession void," was moderate in tone — even conciliatory towards the seceding States. But the South would not be propitiated; the bombardment and capture of Fort Sumter quickly followed Mr. Lincoln's accession to power, and in a few weeks from the time of his inauguration he found himself involved in all the hard, trying conditions of a civil war — a terrible and prolonged contest, which extended over the whole of the first term of his administration, and tested him as rarely any other man was ever tried in the place of exalted leadership.

As the war progressed he had to pass upon perplexing questions connected with slavery. It seemed to some of his friends that he was over-cautious, and did not quickly enough seize the opportunity of profiting by the help of the enslaved population of the seceding States. He would not allow his commanders in the field to issue proclamations declaring freedom to the slaves. He was disposed at the first to compensate the States which would adopt a plan for the gradual and voluntary abolition of slavery; but he was watchful of events and of public opinion, and at the right time he issued the proclamation of emancipation, which, being sustained by the force of arms and subsequent legislation, resulted in the removal of slavery from the Republic.

The unexpected prolongation of the war, the vast expense of treasure and life by which it was carried on, together with political complications and clashing material interests, caused much criticism of the President and his administration. He was very patient under the burden of care and responsibility, and the added load of harsh, mistaken judgment often laid upon him. The great majority of the loyal people were in sympathy with him and rallied to his support, so that he was triumphantly elected to a second term, upon which he entered just as the war was drawing to a close. General Lee surrendered to General Grant April 9, 1865, and this was practically the end of the war. Now that victory was assured to the national government, the hope of President Lincoln was to do a blessed work of reconstruction, building anew the shattered fabrics of seceding States and so causing the restored Union to stand fair and strong. His was the great heart to do this work "with malice toward none, with charity for all." This purpose he was not to realize. His mortal mission was accomplished. He died April 15, 1865, from the effects of an assassin's bullet, honored and mourned by the great body of the American people.

And so this noble, true soul, this strong-minded, great-hearted man passed hence to his reward. His place is assured among the illustrious leaders of the Republic. He represents democracy in its finest instincts. He is a grand, attractive model for individual character and for national life. It is a suggestive picture of the honored, martyred Lincoln which Mr. Lowell draws: "I have seen the wisest statesman and most pregnant speaker of the generation, a man of humble birth and ungainly manners, of little culture beyond what his own genius supplied, become more absolute in power than any monarch of modern times, through the reverence of his countrymen for his honesty, his wisdom, his sincerity, his faith in God and man, and the nobly humane simplicity of his character."

ANDREW JOHNSON.

SEVENTEENTH PRESIDENT OF THE UNITED STATES.

ANDREW JOHNSON.

PRESIDENT, APRIL. 15, 1865 — MARCH 4, 1869.

HUMBLE BIRTH — EARLY MARRIAGE — POPULARITY AMONG HIS TOWNSMEN —
CHOSEN TO FILL SEVERAL PUBLIC OFFICES — MILITARY GOVERNOR OF TEN-
NESSEE — ELECTED VICE-PRESIDENT ON THE TICKET WITH ABRAHAM LIN-
COLN — PRESIDENT OF THE MOURNING NATION — DISAPPOINTING ADMINIS-
TRATION — IMPEACHMENT — REMAINING YEARS AND DUTIES — UNFULFILLED
POSSIBILITIES OF AN HEROIC NATURE.

ASSOCIATED together in the political campaign of 1864 were the names of Lincoln and Johnson, nominated for the respective offices of President and Vice-President. The former was the well-tried leader and statesman, named by the Republican party for a second term in the high office whose duties he had ably discharged; the latter, less known and experienced, a representative of the Southern States, who had given an unwavering support to the Union, and shown a general sympathy with the principles of the party that placed him in nomination. The tragic event which followed so soon the induction of these men into the offices to which they had been elected, was not foreseen. Had it been, perhaps the nominating convention would have hesitated in selecting Andrew Johnson as candidate for Vice-President, from which position, a few weeks after his inauguration, in consequence of the assassination of Mr. Lincoln, he was advanced as the constitutional successor of the Chief Executive,

10

and thus became the seventeenth President of the United States.

Born in Raleigh, North Carolina, December 29, 1808, he shared the common poverty and illiteracy of that district in the beginning of the nineteenth century. The dull monotony of his boyhood was only relieved by the force with which he applied himself to every pursuit, his ardent attention giving a flavor of interest to the daily round of severe tasks imposed by conditions and surroundings. His early marriage brightened his existence, not only by appealing to his affections, but also by awakening his intellectual powers, as the young wife became a teacher, instructing her husband how to write and cipher, he already having learned to read by his own diligent, persevering efforts, unaided by personal instruction.

With this rudimentary education, Andrew Johnson, then living in Greenville, Tennessee, working at his trade, that of a tailor, began to feel an interest in public affairs, and to take somewhat prominent position in local political matters. He identified himself with a workingmen's party which helped in his election, first, as an alderman, and afterwards mayor of the small town where he lived. He was chosen in 1835 a member of the State Legislature, was elected State Senator in 1841, and the year 1843 entered Congress, where he served by successive elections a period of ten years. After fulfilling these important duties he was twice elected Governor of Tennessee, in 1853 and 1855, doing excellent service for his State while occupying the gubernatorial chair. His election to the United States Senate occurred in 1857. Although he gave his support to the general policy of the Democratic party, agreeing with many of the Southern politicians that Congress had no authority to limit the territorial extension of slavery, he opposed the idea of secession, and expressed, in all his speeches in the Senate, an unfaltering support of the Union.

Upon his return to Tennessee Mr. Johnson endeavored to establish a Union party in the State in accordance with the principles he had advocated, arousing great feeling and many threats against him from the adherents of secession. In the year 1862 President Lincoln made the appointment of Andrew Johnson as Military Governor of Tennessee, a position requiring executive ability, cool judgment and prompt action. Beginning his labors in Nashville, soon a besieged city, Governor Johnson's course in dealing with the disheartened Unionists and the desperate secessionists won for him an enviable reputation in the North, and probably led to his nomination for the office of Vice-President. His bold, determined course against secession and its producing cause, now allied him to the Republican party, though he had supported Breckenbridge, the Democratic candidate for the presidency, in the election of 1860, which had resulted in the defeat of that candidate and the preferment of President Lincoln. The personal hardships endured so bravely by Governor Johnson, while in Nashville, his forced separation from family and friends, his hostility to slavery, openly declared, his devotion to his country's interests, gave him prominence as one of the leaders in the Republican party, and showed him to be a strong man for any public position.

Inaugurated as Vice-President, March 4, 1865, it was only a few weeks later that he was called to fill the high office as Chief Magistrate of a people mourning for the hero cruelly murdered by the hand of an assassin. It was about two and one-half hours after the death of President Lincoln that Mr. Johnson took the oath of office, administered to him by Chief Justice Chase, and entered upon the duties of President of the United States. A sorely-stricken and greatly-bereaved people, just emerging from a long and terrible, but now successful war, looked to him in confidence, believing that he would prove a worthy successor to the martyred Lincoln, whose wisdom and patriotism were now set before their vision in clearest lines. A few days after he had assumed the duties of his new position, while the body of the dead President was yet unburied, Mr. Johnson, in response to a delegation from Illinois that called upon him, made a vigorous denunciation of treason as a " crime that must be punished," and intimated his purpose to use strong, if not severe, measures in dealing with all enemies of the government. The sentiments thus avowed were received with marked favor by the loyal people of the land, who felt that their interests were quite safe in the hands of a man cherishing such sentiments. He seemed to represent a quality of manhood that was specially required in dealing with the perplexing questions of reconstruction, and with other problems presented as an inheritance of the long and terrible Civil War. There was hardly a doubt but that President Johnson would be in harmony with a Republican Congress as to the course to be pursued in dealing with the States lately in secession, and all collateral matters related to the policy of the government. To the surprise of Congress and the people, however, President Johnson soon made a manifestation of some of the idiosyncracies of his nature, revealing the fact that he was self-willed and opinionated, stubborn to a fault, and reckless of consequences, however honest he might be at heart.

The picture that is presented of President Johnson at this period, when he stood in opposition to the party to which he owed his election — a Republican Congress, and the great mass of loyal people — is not altogether pleasant to look upon, and yet there are some lines of light let in upon the view. The President might show a sudden and mysterious change of opinion in the matter of dealing with the Southern States; he might approve of measures favored by those who had been

supposed to sympathize more or less with secession; he might
pursue a line of public policy regarded as most detrimental to
the country's interests; yet there he stood, a brave, capable,
not unpatriotic man, who would both avow and maintain his
ideas at any cost. He compels a measure of respect for the
position he took, however mistaken it was, and much to be
deplored as was the antagonism that grew up between the
President and Congress, resulting at last in a movement for
his impeachment.

It is not required, nor does it come within the scope of a
biographical sketch, that these causes of dissension should be
noted in their order, or any opinion passed upon the opposing
theories of reconstruction. The fact, briefly stated, is this:
President Johnson held that the Southern States were never
legally out of the Union, their ordinances of secession being
void, and therefore he thought they were entitled to resume at
once their former relations to the government. Congress held
otherwise, taking the ground that, while the acts of secession
were void, the States which had sought to break away from the
Union should be required to legislate in a certain manner and
offer certain guarantees before being allowed to enter again
upon the enjoyment of all their privileges and have representation in the councils of the Nation. Just here was the vital
point of antagonism. The President vetoed bill after bill passed
by Congress in relation to reconstruction matters, but generally these measures were enacted into laws by a constitutional
majority over the vetoes.

In the elections of 1866, the policy of Congress was approved by the votes of the people, and henceforth the President was placed at a greater disadvantage; but he would not
yield. Congress made an effort to limit the functions of his
authority in the matter of removing officers. Refusing to conform to the provisions of such a Congressional enactment, and

making an attempt to remove Secretary Stanton after the Senate had refused to approve, President Johnson precipitated a crisis which tested again the strength and stability of American institutions. The House of Representatives, on February 24, 1868, passed a resolution impeaching him for high crimes and misdemeanors. He was tried by the Senate, as the Constitution provides, on the charges thus preferred; but, as less than two-thirds of the members of that body voted to sustain the charges, he was acquitted, and continued to serve as President until the end of his term.

The administration of President Johnson was characterized by many important events attesting the progress of national life and influence. Nebraska, formed out of the Louisiana purchase, and concerning the territorial condition of which there had been so much of political dispute, was admitted as a State in 1867, and during the same year the vast region of Alaska was purchased from Russia at a cost of more than seven million dollars.

On March 4, 1869, President Johnson retired from his official responsibilities and duties at the White House, taking up his residence as a private citizen at Greenville, Tennessee. He did not cease, however, to manifest an interest in public affairs, and he was still a somewhat influential factor in political matters of State concern. In January, 1875, the legislature of Tennessee elected him to the Senate of the United States, and he was about to re-enter public life when the summons came to him to pass on and join the silent majority. He died July 31, 1875.

Called to fill the Executive chair at so trying a time in the history of the Nation, succeeding the honored Lincoln whose assassination had wounded every true-hearted citizen the world over, President Johnson bore himself with a degree of courage, with a reliance upon his right convictions that cannot fail to awaken something of admiration for his inherent strength of character. Personally, his features were commonplace, his bearing unostentatious; he was always inclined to bring into prominence the fact of his plebeian origin, yet he had a native force of character which gave dignity to his presence, and he impressed the beholder as an heroic exponent of whatever should appeal to his best judgment. He had sparse opportunities to cultivate friendships, for his entire life was a struggle, with few quiet periods or untroubled hours. The White House sheltered Mrs. Johnson but for a brief time, and, though her daughters were graceful and liberal in their hospitalities, it was not the scene of social amenities or friendly pleasures under the administration of President Johnson. He had the possibilities of a more sympathetic nature than he ever displayed, but the calls for courage and the sterner virtues were so urgent that there was little time for the cultivation of more graceful, attractive, personal qualities. The right estimate to be placed upon one who has been severely criticised, and who certainly made many lapses in the way which he undeviatingly pursued, is suggested by a sentence from a modern writer, giving an account of a personal interview with Mr. Johnson: "I left him with the conviction that, however impolitic or misguided might be his course, a more honest-hearted man did not exist; nor could I believe that the indomitable courage and persistency in behalf of principle which had characterized his conduct before the war, and had made the country ring with the name of 'Andy Johnson,' had become debased by truckling to the sycophancy of disloyal Southern politicians."

ULYSSES S. GRANT.

ULYSSES S. GRANT.

PRESIDENT, MARCH 4, 1869 — MARCH 4, 1877.

HIS OHIO BIRTHPLACE — WEST POINT MILITARY ACADEMY — IN THE MEXICAN WAR — LIFE ON THE FRONTIER — FARMING, AND IN THE LEATHER BUSINESS — HONORABLE RECORD IN THE CIVIL WAR — MANY VICTORIES — PROMOTION TO THE RANK OF MAJOR-GENERAL — PRESIDENT FOR TWO TERMS — HIS ADMINISTRATION — CENTENNIAL — DEATH AFTER MONTHS OF SUFFERING — THE WATCHWORDS OF HIS CAREER.

T HE marginal notes in a printed volume are often necessary to make the text complete and convey the information intended by the writer in his conception of the work. So, in the narrative of a notable career, the side issues, the minor incidents of the life ought at least to be suggested, otherwise a biography, emphasizing only the one heroic act or successful achievement, but inadequately presents the individual, the development of personal qualities and distinguishing characteristics. It is no easy task for the biographer to avoid simply eulogistic writing, to withstand the temptation of dwelling upon well-known events in the human history which he is considering, to clearly bring out the less important details which contributed, however, to the shaping of a career and the moulding of personal qualities. To condense, in a brief sketch, the record of one prominent and useful as Ulysses S. Grant, eighteenth President of the United States, is difficult, indeed, and a limited space almost entirely precludes allusion to the interesting marginal notes, interspersed throughout a life so pregnant with honor and activity.

On the borderland of the great Northwest, in one of Ohio's undeveloped settlements, Point Pleasant, Clermont County, April 27, 1822, a son was born to Jesse Root Grant and his wife, Hannah Simpson. Hiram Ulysses Grant was the name given the boy, but on his entrance to West Point, the official documents, by some mistake, christened him Ulysses Sydney Grant, afterwards changed to Ulysses Simpson, which was adopted by the lad, who was commonly designated "Uncle Sam" by his boyish associates. His father's occupation, that of a tanner, was not congenial to Ulysses, who after strenuous efforts on the part of his friends, secured an appointment to West Point United States Military Academy, where he was an earnest student, but displayed no brilliant mental qualities in any branch of learning which he pursued. His rank on graduating in 1843 was twenty-one in a class of thirty-nine, and his assignment to the Fourth Regiment, then stationed in Missouri, was as second lieutenant in the infantry. He accompanied this regiment to Louisiana, where it was sent in anticipation of troubles arising from this proposed annexation of Texas, and at a little later period took active part in the Mexican War. Serving under General Taylor, and afterwards under General Winfield Scott, Lieutenant Grant was always obedient to his superior officers, prompt to fulfill all duties, never murmured at the hardships of army life, and endured its discipline in the spirit of a true soldier. He was twice promoted for gallantry on the field of battle, and, at the close of the war, he held a Captain's commission. On his return from Mexico, in 1848, he was married to Miss Julia Dent, of St. Louis, and with his wife he spent nearly four years at various ports and garrisons where he was assigned for duty. He was then sent to the Pacific Coast, Mrs. Grant being unable to accompany her husband in his transfer to this distant post of duty. While stationed at Fort Vancouver he was appointed to a captaincy and given another assignment; but he declined further service in the army, resigned his commission in July, 1854, and returned to St. Louis, where his wife and children were then residing.

Captain Grant was now thirty-five years of age, a strong, resolute man, showing some marked peculiarities of mind and character. He had gained large experience by events and associations, and was seemingly fitted for a more prominent career than that which he entered upon when he left the army and settled down to a farmer's life near St. Louis. He applied himself diligently to the pursuits of agriculture, but he was not successful in his new avocation. Then he tried a real estate and collection business, for which he had no liking, and from which he soon withdrew. After experimenting with several other occupations he removed to Galena, Illinois, where he became associated with his father and brothers in the leather business. This was in the early part of the year 1860. Here he lived a quiet, uneventful life until the breaking out of the Civil War. He attended to the commonplace duties which claimed his attention, held himself a good deal in reserve, formed few acquaintances, took no active part in political affairs, and was comparatively unknown in the community.

The war for the Union opened a new career for this quiet man; it gave opportunity for the real quality of his nature to declare itself, and brought into expression hitherto hidden traits of character. With the breaking out of hostilities Grant felt that he had no choice but to offer his services to the National Government. He had received a military training; he was in the full maturity of his strength; he was moved in all the earnestness of a noble nature to contribute some help for the preservation of the Union, and therefore he promptly tendered his services to the authorities, proposing "to act until the close of the war in such capacity as may be offered."

He was first assigned to the work of organizing some of the Illinois volunteers, and afterwards, for a brief period, was connected with the Adjutant-General's office in Springfield, of that State. Grant wanted a place of activity in the field, however, and on June 16, 1861, he was commissioned as Colonel of the Twenty-first Illinois infantry. At once he secured the confidence of officers and men. He showed military capacity by soon bringing his regiment up to a notable condition of discipline and efficiency. He was promoted to the rank of Brigadier-General, being honored with a commission dated May 17, 1861. General Grant was now called to one and another position of importance, where he was subjected to various trials and tests, under which he made ample proof of energy and military skill. General Grant's capture of Fort Henry and Fort Donelson in February, 1862, added greatly to his reputation, while the plan of the movement gave proof of the fact that he had a wise and far-seeing vision as to strategic positions and the various combinations essential to an aggressive warfare.

General Grant, after the successes noted, was advanced in rank, being commissioned by President Lincoln as Major-General. After this preferment, however, he was subjected to harsh criticisms, and for a time was without a command. Only for a brief period, however, was he held to inactivity, for, being restored to his place, he was soon displaying his characteristic energy in organizing and moving his troops for an impending conflict. Whether or not the terrible assault upon the Union army at Shiloh was in any sense a surprise to General Grant, is not made clear; but there can be no question of the fact that this battle was one of the great engagements of the war, with most important issues depending on its result. During the two days' engagement the generalship of Grant was conspicuous. He handled his troops skilfully, he infused confidence into officers and men, he never lost heart himself as to the result.

Following the battle of Shiloh, the capture of Corinth, and other movements by the army of the Tennessee, General Grant advanced upon Vicksburg, then regarded as "the Gibraltar of the Mississippi." After a protracted siege, this Confederate stronghold was surrendered to General Grant on July 4, 1863. It was a signal victory, leading to important results. General Pemberton surrendered an army of about thirty-two thousand men, with one hundred and seventy-two cannon and thousands of small arms. The surrender of Fort Hudson followed in a few days, and thenceforth, as President Lincoln said, "the Mississippi went unvexed to the sea." The fall of Vicksburg caused rejoicing in all the loyal States, while the hearts of the people were moved in sympathetic, grateful accord toward the successful commander whose operations against the fortified city have often been compared to the brilliant movements of Napoleon at Ulm. Advanced to the rank of Major-General in the regular army and placed in command of the newly created Division of the Mississippi, General Grant soon gave additional proof of his possession of the attributes of successful military leadership. He massed his forces at vital points, forced the blockade at Chattanooga, directed several movements in such a way as to secure the desired results, and fought and won the notable battle of Missionary Ridge.

It does not seem surprising, after the brilliant results attending his military campaign in the West, that General Grant should have been called to Washington a few months later and placed in command of all the armies of the United States. His merits were now generally recognized. Congress had revived the grade of Lieutenant-General — a rank held only by Washington and Scott — for the purpose of conferring upon him a superior mark of distinction, and thus grandly augmenting his power. Thenceforth his hand guided the great forces of the war until a successful issue was reached. He led the army of the Potomac against General Lee, fought many hard battles, pushed the enemy from one point to another, at last compelled the evacuation of Petersburg and Richmond, which brought about the surrender of General Lee, an event that practically ended the war. General Grant's magnanimous course in dealing with a brave and conquered foe, at the time of the surrender at Appomattox, April 9, 1865, reveals a breadth of mind and a generosity of feeling which were alike conspicuous elements in his nature.

The close of the war, followed all so quickly and sadly by the assassination of President Lincoln, brought many new duties to the hands of General Grant, who, in the rehabilitation of the regular army, was placed at its head, to the general satisfaction of the soldiers and the people. He gave wise and energetic attention to all matters thus placed in his charge, holding himself aloof, so far as possible, from the political complications that characterized President Johnson's administration. He showed due respect to the President, but he was too keen, self-reliant and patriotic to take any step in opposition to the will of the people as expressed by Congress.

General Grant's prudent course during this trying period, no less than his military popularity, led to his being placed in nomination, in 1868, by the Republican party, as its candidate for President. He was elected by a large majority, his inauguration, March 4, 1869, commanding more than ordinary interest. On that occasion he said: "I shall on all subjects have a policy to recommend, but none to enforce against the will of the people." In 1872 General Grant was elected for a second term, thus giving to him an administration of eight years. His conduct of public affairs was in the main commendable, his honesty of purpose was freely admitted by those who at times were his unsparing critics. He had not the training of a statesman; he lacked some of the elements essential to a perfect character, and requisite to the largest public service; but as he was, and as he revealed himself in the eight years of his holding the office of President, he gave abundant proof of ability and good sense, united with sincere devotion to his country's interests. His administration was characterized by many striking events — among others those attending the Centennial observances of 1876, especially the noteworthy exposition at Philadelphia, opened by the President, and continued from May to November of the year named.

Upon his retirement from the office of President, General Grant spent some two years in a journey around the world, visiting Europe, India, China, Japan, and other important countries, where he was received with great honor and distinction. On his return to the United States he entered into business, in which he was not successful, in New York City. In 1884 a cancerous disease developed which did not admit of any surgical operation for its mitigation or removal. Under this disease he suffered and languished until death came to his relief. He died at McGregor, New York, July 25, 1885.

The teachings of such a life, imperial in its influence, cannot be overestimated. Biographers have dwelt upon its heroic expression, its brilliant successes, its great powers for the leadership of men; there is also another, the "everlasting," side of character, to be extolled. Early in his manhood General Grant nailed upon the door of his heart that thesis embodied in the words, obedience and work. Quietly, yet continuously, he followed the path where they guided his steps, never forgetting the allegiance which they demanded in the performance of the most humble act, as well as in the great deeds, of a life filled with honorable service.

RUTHERFORD B. HAYES.

NINETEENTH PRESIDENT OF THE UNITED STATES.

RUTHERFORD B. HAYES.

PRESIDENT, MARCH 4, 1877 — MARCH 4, 1881.

A MONG the twenty-two eminent men called to fill the chief place in the Government of the American Nation since its formation, a century and more ago, only two are now living, the present incumbent in office, and ex-President Rutherford Birchard Hayes. The life of Mr. Hayes, though less eventful and conspicuous than were the careers of some of his predecessors in the office of President, has in it many points of interest, and well deserves the attention of his countrymen. It has a suggestive attractiveness, not only because of its connection with public affairs, but likewise for the reason that it presents so clear an expression of attributes fostered by the culture and civilization native to the soil of a prosperous republic.

The nineteenth President of the United States was born at Delaware, Ohio, October 4, 1822. In his boyhood he was subjected to many of the limitations of a frontier settlement, especially in the matter of books and schools. Ohio, however, had already inaugurated a movement for common schools, and

11

laid the foundation of institutions of learning of a higher grade, so that the lad of whom we write found better means and facilities for satisfying his active, enquiring mind, than would have been the case had his life begun in the same locality a quarter of a century earlier. He first attended the schools in the vicinity of his home with a view of preparing himself for an advanced course of instruction. The death of his father seemed likely to frustrate the boy's desire in this respect, but an uncle, Sardis Birchard, becoming interested in the youth, furnished the means to enable him to continue his studies and acquire a liberal education. After attending an academy at Norwalk, Ohio, and a preparatory school at Middletown, Conn., he entered Kenyon College at Gambier, Ohio, graduating therefrom in 1842, some months before the completion of his twentieth year. Having decided that he would enter the legal profession, he became a student in the Law School of Harvard College, at Cambridge, Mass., where he made a good record for ability and industry, besides indicating that he had a strong and steady purpose of mind which would most likely bear him well to the front in any path he might enter upon. After graduating at Cambridge he returned to Ohio, being admitted to the bar in 1845, and commencing the practice of his profession at Marietta.

The professional career of Mr. Hayes was attended by a notable degree of success. His natural and acquired competency was quickly recognized, and his careful attention to the interests of his clients did not pass unnoticed. His law practice increased and his reputation grew accordingly. In the year 1850 he removed to Cincinnati, where, in a broader field, with still greater responsibilities given into his hands, he acquired more of prominence as a lawyer, besides gaining in a remarkable degree the esteem and respect of the community. For several years he filled acceptably the important office of

City Solicitor, evincing, in the discharge of the duties of that position, a carefulness and zeal greatly to his credit. In this service, as in the performance of other like trusts, he made expression of many of those qualities which belong to the upper range of human nature, and are always the sign of a strong and attractive individuality.

In 1861, when the Civil War broke out, Mr. Hayes is presented to view as a strong, well-matured man, who had profited by the culture of books and schools, and not less by the experiences of an active professional and public career. If he had not acquired signal distinction, or become widely known, he was yet regarded in the community where he lived and among a constantly increasing circle of appreciative friends, as a prudent and safe man, intelligent and thoughtful, whose counsels might well be followed in the matters of public concern. Thus his influence was felt on the side of the National Government when all so promptly he offered his services in behalf of the Union. He was first commissioned as Major in the Twenty-third Ohio Infantry, the regiment being assigned to duty in West Virginia. During the first year of the war he saw considerable service, endured many hardships, and gave ample proof that he had in his composition the essential elements of a true soldier. Advanced to the rank of Lieutenant-Colonel, he led his regiment in several engagements, and showed such qualities of military skill as to win another promotion, when he was placed in charge of a brigade. He was made Brigadier-General in 1864, for "gallant and distinguished services" at the battle of Cedar Creek. While it may not be claimed that General Hayes is entitled, either by his military ability or achievements, to rank with the few great commanders of the war, it may yet be said he deserves a place of honor with them, both on account of his patriotic devotion and his gallant deeds. He served until the close of the war with

a true, unwavering determination to do his full duty, participated in several hard-fought engagements, and was wounded
four times.

At the close of the war General Hayes entered upon his
Congressional duties, giving close attention, not only to the
special interests of his constituents, but to other more general
questions, which, at that critical period, assumed an exceptional importance. He was re-elected to Congress in 1866,
and the year following was chosen Governor of Ohio. While
discharging the duties of the last named office, he showed a
rare degree of administrative capacity, and so conducted the
affairs of the State as to merit and receive a large measure of
approval. He was re-elected to a second term in 1869, making
a continuous service of four years — from 1867 to 1871 — in
the Gubernatorial office. At the close of the second term,
having declined to be again a candidate, he resumed the place
and duties of a private citizen, taking up once more many of
the lines of professional interest which for a time had fallen
from his hands. Four years later he was again induced to
allow his name to be placed at the head of the Republican
State ticket, and at the election in October, 1875, he was chosen
Governor of Ohio for a third term.

In the year 1876, memorable as the Centennial year of the
Republic, there came a season of more than usual political
excitement. Both of the great parties were considerably agitated within their own lines as to men and measures. When
the Republican National Convention assembled at Cincinnati,
in June of that year, to nominate candidates for President
and Vice-President, a wide divergence of opinion was found
to exist as to the name that should be placed at the head of the
ticket. When the convention entered upon its session Governor Hayes was hardly mentioned as a candidate, and no
effort had been made to secure support in his behalf. When,

however, several ballots had been taken, resulting in no choice, his nomination was strongly urged, and, by a combination of delegates opposed to Mr. Blaine, such a result was effected on the seventh ballot. Senator William A. Wheeler, of New York, was named for the Vice-Presidency, this ticket being opposed, in the exciting political campaign that followed, by the Democrats, who put in nomination Samuel J. Tilden, of New York, and Thomas A. Hendricks, of Indiana.

When the election took place, in November, 1876, the first announcements of results seemed to justify belief in the success of Mr. Tilden; but when the electoral votes came to be counted by Congress it was found that there were conflicting claims in regard to the votes of Florida and Louisiana, without which Mr. Tilden lacked one vote of the number required to elect. If the votes of the two States could be counted for Mr. Hayes his election would be secured. The situation was critical in the extreme. Party feeling ran high, and it almost seemed as though another civil war was impending. The two Houses of Congress, one body having a Republican and the other a Democratic majority, being unable to agree in passing upon the intricate questions involved, decided to refer the whole matter, with full powers, to a Commission composed of five Senators, five Representatives, and five Judges of the Supreme Court. The Commission, after hearing arguments on all the points, decided, by a vote of eight to seven, that the official returns of the State authorities must be accepted as final, thus obliging Congress to count the votes of Louisiana and Florida on the Republican side. This being done, Mr. Hayes was declared to be elected, having received 185 electoral votes to 184 given Mr. Tilden.

The inauguration of the President-elect took place on Monday, March 5, 1877; but in order to guard against any possible contingencies, and that there might be no interregnum from Sunday to Monday in the Presidential office, the necessary oath was administered to Mr. Hayes on Saturday evening, March 3, only a few witnesses being present.

In entering upon the discharge of the duties of his high office Mr. Hayes had to encounter a considerable distrust and ill-feeling, which were natural, in view of the peculiar measures by which his election was established. His bearing at this somewhat trying period, as indeed through all the long controversy from November to March, showed his possession of the elements of a well-balanced nature. He held himself in a proper reserve, was quiet, dignified, self-contained, and modest in manner and in speech, so that he won respect even from those who were greatly dissatisfied by the action of the Electoral Commission, which resulted in his being seated in the Presidential chair. At the very outset of his administration he gave evidence of his breadth of thought and far-reaching, statesmanlike vision, by adopting a policy of conciliation in dealing with the Southern States. This policy was signified by his appointment of a committee to visit the South and report on the measures needed to restore confidence and good feeling among the people of that section. Agreeably to the views of a majority of this committee, and in accordance with his own well-matured thought on the subject, he withdrew the United States soldiers employed in support of the civil officers in several of the States, and prohibited the troops of the General Government from interfering with elections. The character of President Hayes is nowhere better defined or more attractively shown than in his firm adherence to this policy of conciliation and fair treatment to the South. It brought him into direct opposition with many of the leaders of the Republican party; but time has justified his course in this respect, and the American people of to-day will generally applaud, rather than condemn, his action in dealing with the Southern States.

The administration of President Hayes, while not specially brilliant, stands out to view as eminently reputable and clean; an administration characterized by many notable events and attractive features. It presents a wise and economical management of the various branches of the Government, reflecting credit upon the thought and purpose of the Executive, whose influence was acknowledged in all departments. The first steps in civil service reform were taken; foreign affairs were well managed; a new treaty was made with China; the laws protecting the public domain were well enforced; material interests were fostered; specie payments resumed; and thus, as in various other ways by which the progress and prosperity of the country were helped, or signified, the fact was declared that Mr. Hayes had brought a good store of ability, energy and moral purpose to the discharge of the duties of the Presidential office. In this connection it may be mentioned that during the four years from 1877 to 1881 the White House was admirably presided over, in its social affairs, by Mrs. Lucy Webb Hayes, an accomplished and much respected lady to whom the President was married December 31, 1852. The twenty-fifth anniversary of the marriage was observed at the White House, a large number of distinguished guests being present on the occasion.

When Mr. Hayes retired from the Presidential office he returned to his pleasant Ohio home, where he still resides. Although he holds himself aloof from active participation in matters of a merely political nature, he yet engages in much good work related to education, philanthropy and matters of social and moral reform. Thus he finds much of the zest of life as the years of a vigorous and useful age accumulate.

JAMES A. GARFIELD.

TWENTIETH PRESIDENT OF THE UNITED STATES.

JAMES A. GARFIELD.

PRESIDENT, MARCH 4, 1881 — SEPTEMBER 19, 1881.

DISTINGUISHED ANCESTRY — POVERTY AND STRUGGLES IN BOYHOOD — RESOLUTE
PURPOSE TO ACQUIRE AN EDUCATION — A SUCCESSFUL TEACHER — A PREACHER
AND A LAWYER — ENTRANCE INTO POLITICS — MILITARY CAREER — A LEADER
IN CONGRESS — ELECTED PRESIDENT — BRIEF ADMINISTRATION — STRUCK
DOWN BY AN ASSASSIN — STRUGGLE FOR LIFE — THE END — A NOBLE CHAR-
ACTER.

HUMAN greatness is sometimes signified by a single controlling trait of excellence, or by a notable event, perhaps a series of events, with which the individual is associated. There are historic characters and heroic lives which
are attractive by reason of manifestations that are thus exceptional. One bright, noble element of being atones for many
defects; an occasional service, conspicuous and honorable, glo-
rifies the whole life, though a close scrutiny may reveal much
that is wanting in the complete record. But in other cases the
revelation of human greatness appears of a less fragmentary
order; there is seen to be a beautiful combination of the virtues
and graces which most ennoble character, while the whole life
bears witness to the rich and potent forces that control it. To
the class last named belongs the subject of this sketch, James
A. Garfield, the twentieth President of the United States. His
is the strong, full formed, symmetrical character, attractive as a
whole not less than by its distinctive elements, and his is the
growing, productive life, interesting at every point of its expression.

Among the pioneer settlers in that part of Ohio known as the Western Reserve were Abram Garfield and his wife, Elizabeth Ballou Garfield. They were married in Zanesville, Ohio, in 1819, the bridegroom being but twenty years and the bride but eighteen years of age. They began life for themselves in a very humble way, making a clearing in the forest at Newberg, Cuyahoga County, where they established their home in a comfortable log cabin, according to what was the custom in that frontier region. In the year 1830 they removed, with several children that had been born to them, to Orange Township, in the same county, where they made another home on a farm of eighty acres, most of it uncleared land, and entered courageously upon the work and struggles incident to a poor farmer's life, in what was then considered the far West. There in the rude log house, on what seemed to be the outer line of civilization, James A. Garfield was born November 19, 1831.

He was born to a condition of poverty — a condition set about by many limitations, which of necessity would involve the boy in hard struggles. He had an inheritance, however, both on his father's and mother's side, which helped him to break through the limitations of outward condition and make for himself a noble, successful career. His father was a man of energy and intelligence, imbued with an honest, manly purpose of life. He was descended from good Puritan stock that came to Massachusetts Colony with Winthrop in 1630. "Each of the six generations that dwelt in Massachusetts," says Mr. Hoar, "has left an honorable record still preserved." On his mother's side, also, the subject of this sketch could claim this best sort of inheritance. His mother, New Hampshire born, was a direct descendant of Maturin Ballou, a prominent Huguenot who fled from France, after the revocation of the edict of Nantes, to a home of freedom in Rhode Island. From such an ancestry James A. Garfield derived much of native force of character and essential preparation for the important station he was to fill.

His boyhood life was somewhat hard and unpromising. He was but a babe when his father died, leaving four children to the care of the faithful mother, who applied herself with the utmost of energy and courage to the support of her dependent household. She wrought with her hands in the house and in the fields to provide for them ; but while thus held to burdensome toil she found time to train the minds of her children and help them in obtaining the first acquisitions of learning. James had a strong will, a cheerful temper, an acute moral sensibility, was resolute to maintain his rights, but most ready to be fair and just to others. When sixteen years old he left home to seek employment. He engaged in different kinds of labor, being employed for some months as a driver of horses upon the tow-path of the Pennsylvania and Ohio Canal. This kind of work was not congenial to the thoughtful, studious youth, and on his return home, prompted by his mother's advice, he determined to obtain an education and strike out for a more ambitious course.

In the year 1849 young Garfield became a student in Geauga Seminary, located in Chester, a few miles away from his childhood's home. For two years and more he attended this academy, not continuously, however, for he was forced to take long vacations in which he wrought with his hands or taught school, in order to obtain the means to pay tuition fees and supply himself with books.

In the fall of 1851 he entered the Hiram Institute, at Hiram, Ohio, where he was both pupil and instructor. In 1854 he was admitted to the junior class of Williams College, at Williamstown, Mass., graduating therefrom with highest honors two years later. While a member of these institutions his cheerful disposition, genial manners, and general uprightness of demeanor, gained for him a large measure of esteem. His capacity for study was marvellous and his diligence untiring. He was fond of athletic sports and social life; but the intellectual part of his being was in the ascendancy, so that he left college with an excellant reputation for literary scholarship and general culture.

This was James A. Garfield as he is presented to view when twenty-three years of age, at the time of his leaving college and entering upon the more active and responsible duties of life. Accepting the position of Professor of Ancient Languages in the Hiram Institute, he taught successfully for some two years, when he was elected its President. He administered the larger trust with general satisfaction, finding time in addition to his routine engagements for wide and varied reading and the giving of some attention to political affairs. For a time, during 1857–8, he preached almost every Sunday, having joined the Communion of Disciples, and being much interested in religious work; then he studied law, being admitted to the bar after due examination. His activity in politics began with the Fremont campaign of 1856, at which period he made a number of public addresses, discussing the issues involved, and advocating the election of General Fremont. By these addresses he became more widely known, and the way was opened to increased political activity and prominence, resulting, in the year 1859, in his election to the Ohio Senate, where his ability as a leader was quickly recognized. A year previously, on November 11, 1858, he had married Miss Lucretia Rudolph, whom he first met at Geauga Seminary, and to whom he was engaged before his entering college.

Mr. Garfield participated in the exciting campaign of 1860, rendering an able service on the platform in behalf of the principles of the Republican party. He rejoiced at the election of

Mr. Lincoln, and when, soon after his inauguration, the President issued a call for 75,000 men to uphold the Union, the influence of Senator Garfield was an important factor in the Ohio Legislature in determining the prompt response that was made by that body to the appeal. Having declared his purpose of entering the field, he was commissioned by Governor Dennison, August 14, 1861, as Lieutenant-Colonel of the Forty-Second Regiment Ohio Volunteers. Two days later he was mustered into service, entering upon a military career for which he had no special training, although he brought to the discharge of the new duties a well-trained mind, a quick and comprehensive judgment, and an ardent love of the Union. While holding the rank of Colonel he was placed in charge of a brigade of soldiers, and conducted important operations in eastern Kentucky. His zeal and ability thus shown won for him a promotion to the rank of Brigadier-General. He took part in the battle of Shiloh; was a member of several military courts, notably the one convened in Washington for the trial of General Porter; served as Chief of Staff to General Rosecrans, and bore a leading part in the battle of Chickamauga, being promoted to a Major-Generalship for his gallant conduct in that engagement.

Practically, the military career of General Garfield ends at this point, for obedient to a sense of duty, he decided to resign his commission in the army and accept a place as Representative in Congress, to which he had been chosen, in his absence, by the voters of the Nineteenth Ohio District. He entered Congress in 1863, being continued there by successive elections for nearly seventeen years, and making the mark of his keen, incisive thought upon much of the legislation of that period. He made a clear showing of the qualities that characterize an able party leader, as likewise of those higher gifts which belong to the statesman. Mr. Blaine, in his eulogy on

President Garfield, delivered February 27, 1882, paid him a
high tribute, declaring "that no one of the generation of public men to which he belonged has contributed so much that
will be valuable for future reference. His speeches are numerous, many of them brilliant, all of them well studied, carefully phrased, and exhaustive of the subject under consideration." In another portion of the eulogy, reference is made to
the comprehensiveness of Mr. Garfield's mind, and his far-
reaching political vision, as shown by his speeches in Congress.
"His speeches forecast many great measures yet to be com-
pleted — measures which he knew were beyond the public
opinion of the hour, but which he confidently believed would
secure popular approval in due time." He was always influential in Congress, and in the later terms of his service he
was the foremost leader of the Republican party in the House
of Representatives.

In the early part of 1880, General Garfield was elected
United States Senator from Ohio; but before he had resigned
his seat in the House to enter upon the higher position he received the Republican nomination for the Presidency. This
nomination came to him unsought and unexpected. It was
after two days' undecisive balloting that his name was brought
forward against his own protest, and the Convention turned
to his support. The result of the campaign that followed was
his election over General Hancock, the Democratic candidate,
by a considerable majority. He was inaugurated President
of the United States on March 4, 1881.

The view presented of President Garfield at that time is
certainly an attractive one. He was in the prime of life, well
versed in the science of government, a man of large and varied attainments, favorably known as a scholar and a statesman, and specially fitted by these acquisitions, as by the intellectual and moral tone of his life for the exalted office he was

called to fill. The hearts of the people went out to him in great confidence, the general feeling being that under his guidance all departments of the public service would be wisely directed, and the interests of the whole country promoted. Thus President Garfield started out upon the seemingly bright course before him; he showed statesmanlike qualities in dealing with difficult questions, but the few months of his administration were insufficient to develop his purposes and plans. While in the midst of his exalted usefulness he was struck down by the bullet of an assassin, receiving a wound that caused his death after eighty days of languishing and suffering. President Garfield was shot at about 9 A. M., on Saturday, July 2, 1881, while in the waiting room of the Baltimore and Potomac Railway Station, in Washington, D. C. On the 7th of September he was removed to Long Branch, where he died on the 19th of the same month, the whole land mourning his fate; the whole civilized world in sympathy with a bereaved people.

The character and services of James A. Garfield ensure to him an honored, grateful remembrance in the hearts of the American people. " Well may we be proud of him, " said Mr. Lowell, "this brother of ours, recognized also as a brother wherever men honor what is praiseworthy in man. Well may we thank God for him, and love more the country that could produce and appreciate him." Fortunate is that nation whose heroes are compounded of such excellent qualities! Fortunate a people privileged to look upon the true types of manly greatness, as witnessed by those who have filled exalted stations, and been all so diligent in serving their country's interests and helping the world to better things!

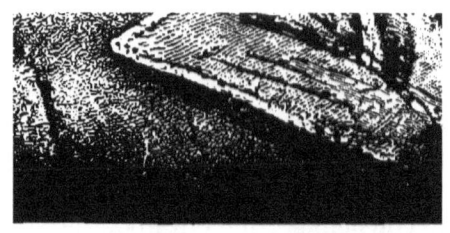

CHESTER A. ARTHUR.

TWENTY-FIRST PRESIDENT OF THE UNITED STATES.

CHESTER A. ARTHUR.

PRESIDENT, SEPTEMBER 19, 1881 — MARCH 4, 1885.

SON OF A NEW ENGLAND CLERGYMAN — A HUMBLE BUT INSPIRING HOME —
SUPPORTS HIMSELF IN SCHOOL AND COLLEGE — NOTABLE TRAITS OF CHAR-
ACTER — ENTERS THE LEGAL PROFESSION — CHAMPIONS THE CAUSE OF COL-
ORED PEOPLE — POLITICAL ACTIVITY — IMPORTANT SERVICES DURING THE
WAR — COLLECTOR OF PORT OF NEW YORK — VICE-PRESIDENT — SUCCESSOR
OF GARFIELD IN THE PRESIDENTIAL OFFICE — THE MAN AND HIS WORK —
DEATH.

TESTS, many and severe, have been applied to the organic
life of the United States. The strength of the Republic has been shown by the endurance of these tests.
Thus four Presidents have died in office, leaving to the Vice-
President the constitutional succession to the first place in the
government; and such succession has been accomplished without undue excitement, and with no interruption to general prosperity. It was the fourth instance of so critical a change when
Chester A. Arthur was called to the office of Chief Magistrate,
having trusts and duties thus devolved upon him quite unlike
those attached to the position to which he had been elected.

In tracing the early career of the twenty-first President of
the United States, we are led to the humble abode of a Bap-
tist clergyman in Fairfield, Vermont. Rev. William Arthur,
father of the subject of the present sketch, came to this country from the North of Ireland some two or three years before
he had attained his majority. Although his talents were not

12

conspicuous, he was intelligent and well educated. He ministered to parishes in Vermont and New York, wrote several treatises on religious subjects, and was actively interested in antiquarian and genealogical pursuits. He died in Newtonville, New York, in the year 1875. It was while settled as pastor at Fairfield, Vermont, that his son Chester was born— on October 5, 1830. The Vermont birthplace was of a very unpretending character. There was, however, a homely charm to the spot; with something of education in the picturesque surroundings. Early in the boy's life his father moved to Troy, New York, where better advantages in the way of books and schools were available. The lad in the fifteenth year of his age was so far advanced in his studies, that he had no trouble in being admitted to Union College, Schenectady, New York, where he graduated in 1848. Notwithstanding his youth, he supported himself in part during his college course by teaching school. He is remembered as a young man of ready speech and winning manners, whose influence in the community was remarkable for one whose years were so few.

After graduating from Union College Mr. Arthur continued to teach as opportunity offered; he also applied himself to a prescribed course of reading and study, with a view of preparing himself for the legal profession. Having accumulated, by diligence and economy, a few hundred dollars, he went to New York City, and there entered upon a more ambitious course of activity and usefulness. Admitted to the bar in 1853, he was, within a year from that date, given a share in the law business of Mr. E. D. Culver, the firm name being Culver, Parker and Arthur. The junior member, although but twenty-three years of age, soon found opportunity to make proof of the natural quickness of his mind, and the worth of that careful training which he had received. He gave a close application to his profession, was orderly and business-like in his methods, and gained reputation as an advocate, both as a logical reasoner and for the ability he evinced to bring into use all available resources in his clients' interests.

Early in the professional career of Mr. Arthur he became identified with a case in the courts turning upon the question as to whether or not a slaveholder could take his slaves into a free State and hold them as property while temporarily residing there. Judge Elijah Paine decided that a slave brought voluntarily by his master into New York was free. This judgment was appealed from, and the case was carried into the Supreme Court of the United States, great efforts being made by the slave holding interest to obtain a reversal of the decision. Mr. Arthur made an earnest appeal to the Legislature of New York, that this body should engage counsel to maintain the constitutionality of the laws of the State, and action was taken accordingly, the result being that the original decision was sustained, and the New York statutes relating to this question were pronounced to be in accord with the Constitution. By his interest and zeal shown in this celebrated case, and his readiness to protect the colored people in their legal rights, he advanced his reputation, became more widely known in political circles, and his influence was correspondingly increased.

Mr. Arthur acted with the Whig party in the declining days of that organization. When the Republican party was formed, his sympathies and convictions naturally led him to its support. Nor was he an inactive member. He contributed in essential ways to strengthen the organization, to perfect its plans and make them successful. He was a born organizer, and in the way of skillful arrangement and management, rendered an efficient service to the new party, and made his influence felt outside the lines of the immediate locality where his political activity was most conspicuous. He became popular by reason of his free and genial manners, his sympathetic attitude toward the common people, and the faith and fearlessness he manifested in maintaining whatever interests related to men or measures, that might claim his adherence. In the campaign of 1860 he used his best efforts for the election of Mr. Lincoln, to whose administration he gave cordial support. When the Civil War broke out Mr. Arthur held the place of Engineer-in-Chief on the Staff of Governor Morgan, of New York, and in this official relation to the Chief Executive of that State was called to the exercise of important trusts. Early in 1861 he was placed in charge of a branch of the Quartermaster's department in New York City, given large powers, which were increased with the increasing demands of the Government for military support, until practically he had almost sole charge of preparing and equipping the soldiers of New York for service in the field. In 1861, as Inspector-General, he visited the New York regiments in the Army of the Potomac and administered to their wants. During the same year, as Quartermaster-General of the State, he stimulated the raising of re-inforcements, gave attention to the providing of needed supplies, and took care that there should be no lavish expenditure in the furnishing of these requisites. His services at this time may well be counted for as much on the Union side as though he had been in the field commanding a brigade or an army corps.

In 1863, following the election of Horatio Seymour as Governor, General Arthur retired from these responsible positions and resumed the practice of law in New York City. His interest in public affairs continued unabated, and his hand was upon many important political movements. As Chairman of the Republican State Executive Committee of New York he wielded a potent influence during the political canvass of 1868. He was especially devoted to General Grant, and most heartily did he seek to advance the political interests of that great chieftain, and secure his elevation to the Presidency. Near the close of 1871 President Grant appointed General Arthur to be Collector of the Port of New York, an office for which he had more than ordinary fitness. His management of this responsible trust gave such satisfaction that, when he was re-appointed, on the expiration of his first term, the Senate, by a unanimous vote, confirmed the appointment, without any refer-ence of the matter to a committee. As the outcome of a com-plicated political situation, he was removed from the office of Collector in July, 1878, but this removal was understood to be no reflection upon his integrity, or his generally careful and business-like management of the office he had held for a period of nearly seven years.

The Republican National Convention which met in Chicago in June, 1880, after two days' balloting, selected James A. Garfield as candidate for President, and associated with him, as candidate for Vice-President, the subject of this sketch. In the election that followed these candidates were elected, and their inauguration took place March 4, 1881. As presiding officer of the Senate, Vice-President Arthur gave proof of ability; although altogether without legislative experience, he was dignified, courteous and self-possessed. The severest criticism made against him was the charge of undue political interest and manipulation, as evinced notably in his endeavor to secure the re-election of Roscoe Conkling by the New York Legislature.

From the time of the attempted assassination of President Garfield there seemed to be a marked development of char-acter and responsibility on the part of the Vice-President, who bore himself in an admirable manner during the trying period when the life of the Chief Executive hung trembling in the balance. With the death of the President, September 19, 1881, all the powers of the first office devolved upon Vice-

President Arthur; he took the oath of office on September 20, 1881, and at once entered upon the momentous tasks thus assigned. He made no attempt to frustrate the supposed purposes of President Garfield, but on the contrary avowed his intention to carry out the policy of his predecessor. If in anything he caused disappointment, it was that he proved himself to be less radical and clannish, more broad minded and tolerant, than some had anticipated. His inaugural address, which contained no special reference to the Southern States, gave a clear intimation of a decreasing feeling of sectionalism, and of the putting aside, as belonging to past issues, many of the disturbing questions resulting from slavery.

President Arthur, very soon after his succession to the Chief Magistracy, was called to take part officially in the Centennial celebration of the surrender of Cornwallis, at Yorktown, Virginia, on which occasion there were present, besides the President, members of his Cabinet, Senators, Representatives, Governors of the States, and other prominent officials, together with invited guests from France and Germany, and a large concourse of citizens. Although the nation was but just recovering from the stroke of severe bereavement, this celebration was observed in the heartiest manner, and reference may well be made to it here as one of the notable events with which the President was associated during his term of office.

President Arthur, with skillful hand, gave direction to public interests, making his robust thought and intelligent purpose to be felt in all departments subject to the Executive control. Most certainly he grew in public favor by the course he pursued while holding the Presidential office — by his manifestation of statesmanlike qualities, and not less by his evident purpose to act fairly in respect to all questions on which he was called to pass judgment, and to recognize the claims of all sections of the country and all classes of citizens. For some of his administrative acts he was greatly criticised, but on the whole, he received commendation as one who sought to do his full duty in the exalted office to which he had succeeded. Impressed by his administrative skill shown in the successful guidance of public affairs, his many political friends rallied about the leader they honored and admired and sought to secure for him another term in the Presidential office. He was a candidate before the National Republican Convention of 1884, but failed to obtain the number of votes needed, Mr. Blaine being chosen as the standard bearer of the Republican party in the campaign of that year.

On the 4th of March, 1885, President Arthur retired from the cares and responsibilities which he had sustained for nearly three and a half years as Chief Magistrate of the Republic. On leaving Washington he went to his home in New York City, having the purpose to rest his severely taxed mind and give attention to physical ills which had assumed a somewhat threatening character. The desired renewal of health and strength did not come to him; gradually he grew weaker under the malady which had fastened itself upon his system, until death ensued on November 18, 1886. Thus passed on the spirit of one who presents a character in many respects bright and attractive. President Arthur was a man of culture, broad-minded, sweet-tempered, having a good share of those attributes and characteristics which mark manly worth. He is deserving of remembrance for these things, as well as for the offices he held and the services he rendered.

GROVER CLEVELAND.

TWENTY-SECOND PRESIDENT OF THE UNITED STATES.

GROVER CLEVELAND.

PRESIDENT, MARCH 4, 1885.

NEW ENGLAND ANCESTORS — ASSIDUITY AND ENERGY OF THE LAD — A STRONG
WILL — LAWYER AND POLITICIAN — ELECTED GOVERNOR OF NEW YORK —
BUSINESS METHODS IN OFFICE — PERSONAL BEARING AND CHARACTERISTICS
— ELECTED PRESIDENT — CONDUCT OF PUBLIC AFFAIRS — A WELL-DEFINED
INDIVIDUALITY.

POPULAR government implies the existence of political
parties. Wherever the people are recognized as the
source of power, having in their hands the choice of their
rulers, and a determination of the general course of public
procedure, there must be opposing organizations to represent
differences of opinion respecting important questions and issues.
The parties thus formed exercise checks and balances, without
which popular government would be exposed to greater risks
than ever, while they stimulate men to the discharge of the
duties of intelligent citizenship. It is when the people by
their votes have expressed a judgment respecting men and
measures that the political party thus approved acquires the
control of the Government, for a fixed period, within the lines
marked out by the Constitution.

Parties have existed from the the days of Washington
until now. Since the year 1856 the two opposing organizations have been designated by the respective names Republican and Democratic; these two titles, it should be remembered, having been used formerly with much the same signifi-

cation. The Republican party came into power with the inauguration of Mr. Lincoln in 1861, and continued to be charged
with the administration of the General Government until
March 4, 1885, when the subject of the present paper, Grover
Cleveland, was conducted into the office of President. After
twenty-four years of Republican rule and direction, a change
was effected by the success of the Democratic party in the
campaign of 1884, and a transfer of power from one of the
great political organizations to the other, peacefully accomplished according to the will of the people expressed at the
ballot box.

In preparing a biographical sketch of the man thus chosen
to fill the most exalted office in the gift of his countrymen,
there is no call to review so long and eminent a course of public service preceding such election, as in the case of some of the
occupants of the Presidential chair. Mr. Cleveland came sud-
denly into public favor; his nomination and election to the
office of President appear somewhat remarkable, and most certainly are typical of our time and country. That he was in
many respects well prepared for his elevation to the first place
of public responsibility and duty, is evident, however, to all
who give careful scrutiny to his strongly marked traits of character, the culture and training of his life, and the acquirements
and experiences by which he had so much profited.

Grover Cleveland, like his immediate predecessor in office,
was a minister's son. His father, Rev. Richard F. Cleveland, a
clergyman in the Presbyterian communion, was settled for some
time at Caldwell, Essex County, New Jersey, where the subject of this sketch was born, March 18, 1837. His early home
was a humble one, but favorable to both mental and moral culture. He had a native endowment of no mean order, deriving
a heritage better than material wealth from an illustrious ancestry, whose history began with the coming of Moses Cleveland,

an Englishman, to Massachusetts, in the year 1635. Aaron Cleveland, second son of Moses, and the great-grandfather of the President, was a man of much influence in his day and generation. He was a Congregational clergyman located in Connecticut. His son, the grandfather of Grover, also a resident of Connecticut, was a man much respected. With this bright line of lineage on his father's side, and having an excellent mother, the daughter of Abner Neal, of Baltimore, Maryland, Grover Cleveland entered upon life well equipped for a successful career.

When about four years of age the boy was taken by his parents to Fayetteville, Oneida County, New York, where the father was stationed as a preacher. A little later another removal was made to Clinton, and afterwards to Holland Patent, at which place his father died in 1853. The years of the lad's existence during the time preceding this event were not of an eventful character. He studied some, read a good deal, profited by attending the schools available, and still more by the excellent home instruction he received. With the death of his father came a breaking up of home, a change in conditions and surroundings, which, no doubt, had much to do with shaping the future life of the son. His first engagement was that of a teacher in the New York Institution for the Blind. He was a faithful, patient teacher, applying himself diligently to the duties of the subordinate position he held. With two years of experience thus gained, he started West to find a broader field of opportunity. At the suggestion of an uncle, residing at Buffalo, New York, the young man decided to remain at that city. He entered the law office of Rogers, Bowen and Rogers, worked hard, made rapid progress, so that, being admitted to the bar in 1859, he soon became the managing clerk of the office where he had obtained his professional training. His energy as at that time displayed, his orderly methods of work, his industry, and his earnest, bold expression of a strong individuality, gained for him a large measure of public respect and confidence, while they pointed to a career of honored usefulness.

In the year 1863 Mr. Cleveland was appointed Assistant District Attorney of Erie County, New York, an office which he held some three years. His scrupulous attention to matters of detail was specially noticeable, as well as the completeness of service in any work once entered upon. As Sheriff of the same County, to which position he was elected in 1870, he added to his reputation in the respects indicated. After holding the office of Sheriff for three years he resumed his law practice, becoming professionally associated with Lyman K. Bass and Wilson S. Bissell. At a later period Mr. George J. Sicard was admitted to partnership, the law firm then being designated as Cleveland, Bissell and Sicard. Mr. Cleveland was at this time in the full maturity of his powers, ranked as an able advocate, a self-reliant man, having the courage of his convictions. Thus he was selected, in 1881, to be an exponent of the Reform sentiment in Buffalo; for although nominated as candidate for Mayor by the Democratic party, he was supported and elected on a platform of administrative improvement in municipal affairs. His conduct of public interests while Mayor served to draw him more closely to the friends of good government, and caused his name to be approvingly mentioned, not only in the city and county where he resided, but outside of these local lines. When the Democratic State Convention met in Syracuse, in the fall of 1882, Mr. Cleveland was nominated for the office of Governor, great enthusiasm being expressed in his behalf. His triumphant election followed in November of that year, the popular feeling turning to him far in excess of any mere party approval. No political leader, no candidate for any office, ever succeeded in carrying the people of New York with him, more numerously and more earnestly than did Mr. Cleveland in the memorable election of 1882. His majority of 192,854 votes was unprecedented.

Governor Cleveland signified in his inaugural message, delivered January 2, 1883, some of the underlying features of good government, while he pointed out very distinctly his purpose to exercise a watchful supervision over all departments, thus ensuring, so far as possible, a prudent and economical administration of the State Government. Probably no Governor ever worked harder than he, or exercised a more careful scrutiny in regard to all branches of service more or less directly subject to Executive control. He sought to know the merits of every question upon which he was called to pass official judgment. When he had once reached a decision, however, he was tenacious in maintaining his position. His frequent exercise of the veto power brought him at times into opposition with the Legislature, while his views on public questions were not always in accord with the sentiments of his party. But though subjected to adverse criticism because of his approval or disapproval of certain measures, and not always in harmony with the leaders of the party to which he belonged, Governor Cleveland's course was generally approved; both by his words and acts he made impression upon the people throughout the country, and his place was acknowledged to be among the foremost leaders of the Democratic party.

When the National Convention of the Democratic party met at Chicago, in July, 1884, the name of Grover Cleveland was brought forward for the Presidential nomination. On the second ballot he received the nomination, which afterwards was made unanimous. A political campaign of more than ordinary excitement followed, resulting in his election as President of the United States. He received 219 electoral votes against 182 cast for Mr. Blaine, the candidate of the Republican party.

The inauguration of President Cleveland, March 4, 1885, was on many accounts a memorable occasion. It signified the return of the Democratic party to power in the control of the Executive Department of Government, after an interregnum of twenty-four years. It signified the preferment of a man whose absolute official integrity had never been questioned, and whose administration of the Government, it was generally believed, would be both honest and efficient. The time has not come to pass in review the administration of President Cleveland, the end of whose term of office has not yet been reached, or to estimate without partisan favor or prejudice the acts that have marked his course as Chief Magistrate of the American Nation. It will be conceded that he has given careful attention to the duties of the Presidential office, that he has never sought to avoid work or responsibility, and that he has wrought successfully in many respects, if not in all, in his endeavors to promote the best welfare of the people and maintain the Government in its dignity and its strength. In his messages he has discussed important questions with boldness, and whatever dissent there may be to his recommendations, he will not be likely to suffer in reputation on account of his presentation of living issues in connection with his own plainly avowed opinions. He may have failed in not accomplishing as much in the way of Civil Service Reform as the people anticipated, but he has done something in this direction, as he has always advocated the underlying principles of the laws enacted during late years to improve that service and separate it from the "spoils system" of politics. In his conduct of foreign affairs, also, while there may not have been the desired measure of success in all negotiations carried on, he has shown firmness in upholding American rights under the law, united with an earnest purpose to bring about a satisfactory settlement of any and all questions in dispute.

President Cleveland's administration, now drawing to a close, will be remembered as associated with a period of material prosperity and general good feeling throughout the country. It will be recalled, also, as including a limit within which the people of this country were called to mourn the death of prominent statesmen and great commanders whose services illumine the pages of the Nation's history. Among these, mention may be made of Ex-President Grant, who died July 23, 1885, and whose funeral was attended by President Cleveland, the members of his Cabinet, Generals of the Army, and prominent officials of the Government, together with a mighty concourse of people, all testifying of the Nation's mourning for the dead hero, and its just recognition of the fame of one who will forever live in remembrance as " a great soldier, a faithful public servant, a devoted defender of the public faith, and a sincere patriot."

In writing the closing sentences of this biographical sketch, reference may well be made to an event which has contributed to bring President Cleveland nearer to the hearts of the people and augment his popularity, viz., his marriage to Miss Frances Folsom, which took place June 2, 1886. Mrs. Cleveland has presided over the White House to the great acceptance of visitors and guests, while the way and manner in which she has met all demands of her position, have drawn to her a kindly feeling throughout the country, quite superior to any partisan sentiment. Fortunate, indeed, is the President of the United States thus blessed in domestic companionship, and so strengthened and better prepared to discharge the duties and fulfill the trusts of his exalted official position.

www.ingramcontent.com/pod-product-compliance
Lightning Source LLC
Chambersburg PA
CBHW030611040726
47497CB00008B/2938